Thirteen Ways to Water

Thirteen Ways to Water

and other stories

◆ ◆ ◆

Bruce Holland Rogers

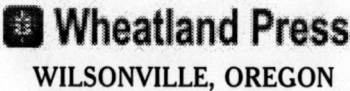
WILSONVILLE, OREGON

PANISPHERE
EUGENE, OREGON

Some of these stories first appeared in *Realms of Fantasy, The Magazine of Fantasy & Science Fiction,* and *Ideomancer.*

Others first saw print in these anthologies:
Black Cats and Broken Mirrors
Earth, Air, Fire, Water: Tales From the Eternal Archives #2
Historical Hauntings
Fantastic Alice
Monster Brigade 3000

"Heart of Shanodin" and "The Brass Man Who Would Sink" were originally published in *Tapestries*, an anthology from Wizards of the Coast. © 1995 Wizards of the Coast, Inc. All rights reserved. **Magic: The Gathering** and **Wizards of the Coast**® are trademarks of Wizards of the Coast, Inc.

THIRTEEN WAYS TO WATER AND OTHER STORIES. Copyright © 2004 by Bruce Holland Rogers. All rights reserved. Printed in the United States of America. No part of this book may be used or reproduced in any manner whatsoever without written permission except in the case of brief quotations embodied in critical articles or reviews. Panisphere Books and Audio, 1485 E. Briarcliff Lane, Eugene, OR 97404-3268.

ISBN 0-9704210-4-4

For Bertram, Lara and Sara

Contents

Thirteen Ways to Water	1
Half of the Empire	17
Whalesong	27
How Golf Shaped Scotland	35
In the Chief's Name	45
Heart of Shanodin	61
A Common Night	99
The Brass Man Who Would Sink	125
Ever So Much	141
In the Matter of the Ukdena	155
Twas the Night Before Global Economic Integration	179
Okra, Sorghum, Yam	185
How the Highland People Came to Be	195

Introduction to "Thirteen Ways to Water"

The title story of this collection was first published in an anthology about superstitions. I decided to write about soldiers, because the battlefield often gives rise to magical thinking. No wonder. In war, the stakes are life-and-death, but the people whose lives are on the line often have very little control over what happens to them. Superstition is an attempt to impose some order on seemingly carpricious fate.

This story won the Nebula Award for 1998.

Thirteen Ways to Water

1. With Blood

When Jack Salter was seventeen two other guys held his arms while Bull Wilson punched his face. Three times. Hard.

"You stay away from Diane," Bull said. "Don't even *talk* to her."

Later, on the river bank, Jack washed the blood from his face and thought, *I'll never forget this. I will never forgive.*

2. Because She Asks Him To

When Diane Wilson comes to Jack this time, it isn't out of the mists of fantasy. She comes in a BMW, and she's her real self, a woman almost fifty.

He's sitting under the overhang of his tin roof when she drives up. The blue Beemer looks strange on the gravel road that generally sees VW bugs or beat-up Hondas or more often no traffic at all. Diane wears a suit and jacket. She goes from crisp to wilted the minute she gets out of the car's air conditioning. He puts down his book but doesn't stand.

"Jack," she says.

He nods but can think of nothing to say that won't seem like a formula. Not, *This is a surprise.* Not, *How've you been?*

The silence grows between them. He thinks it is strange at his age to feel this sort of awkwardness. At last she tells him, "I need your help, Jack."

"My help," he says.

"Actually," she says, "Bull needs your help."

He could laugh then. He could shake his head. He could say, *The son of a bitch you married needs* my *help?* But instead he folds his hands and says, "Tell me."

"He's down by the river," she says. "He's been there for days. I looked and looked and when I found him, he told me it was for the water. So he could drown."

"I don't understand," Jack says.

"I don't either." She begins to cry.

He doesn't stand up, go to her, embrace her. He lets her stand there, wet-faced, hugging herself, shaking, until she is finished. She opens her purse and takes out a tissue.

"Why don't you call the police?"

"I guess you won't do it," she says.

"I didn't say that."

"If I call the police, they'll hospitalize him. We've been through that once. The doctors can't do anything for him. The headaches come right back, and he hates me for doing that, for handing him over like that as if he'd done something."

"What headaches?"

She tells him, then, about the cluster headaches, a dozen attacks some days that make Bull Wilson stalk the floor, wail, beat his fists against his head or his head against the wall. Like fire in his head, like a blade in his skull boring in, digging and scraping.

Like guilt.

No, not guilt. Bull Wilson would never feel guilty.

Jack says, "Why me?"

"He talks about the war. Not to me. But to men—his friends or even strangers who find him there by the river. He tells his war stories. And you were there."

"A lot of men in town were there."

"But you... I just have this feeling about you. About the kind of person you are. Bull's friends can't help him. They don't know what to do."

"And I will?"

She looks at him long and hard. "Maybe."

Jack nods then. He wonders if she knows what he did in the war, if she knows that she is asking him to do it again, thirty years later. Although this won't be the same. This will be altogether different, if he can do it at all.

He says, "I'll try."

3. Under the cottonwoods

He finds Bull Wilson just where Diane says he'll be, crouched among the blackberry brambles along the riverbank, in the shade of black cottonwoods.

Bull still wears his tie, hasn't even loosened it, but three nights of sleeping beside the Willamette have left mud stains on his suit. His hair is a mess. Bull's eyes are red. Veins show on his blistered nose.

Even so, when Jack makes his way through the poison oak, Bull meets him with a blue gaze so steady that Jack thinks for a moment that this will be easy, that he'll just say, as if they were old friends, *Come on, Bull. Let's go home*, and reclaim him.

But the gaze is more than steady. Bull stares. He stares *beyond* Jack. If he knows who Jack is, he gives no sign.

A thin chain is wrapped around Bull's hand like a rosary. A fifty caliber shell dangles from the end.

"Hey, Bull," Jack says.

"Ghosts," Bull whispers. Then he says, "They won't leave me." He pounds his forehead with his fist and shouts, "They won't fucking stop!" He grimaces, keeps hitting himself.

Jack sits down, not too close, and watches the green churn of the Willamette, waits for Bull's headache to pass. He waits for Bull to say the next thing he will say.

4. Downhill

When Jack Salter was a boy, his father showed him the mountains. They hiked the rain-soaked Siskiyous, the big timber of the Cascades, the scrubby Sheepshead Mountains. And his father taught him that if he were lost, he should go the way that water goes. He should follow a slope to a stream, follow the stream to a river, follow the river to safety.

5. Lethe

They were far north of the DMZ, two Jolly Green Giants hovering above the tree tops. They'd had to wait for their Skyraider escort to fly up from Da Nang. That gave the NVA time to locate the pilot, set a trap.

As the Skyraiders circled, Jack rode the cable down, found his man in the underbrush, loaded him onto the litter. When the two of them reached the helicopter doorway, the enemy opened up. A rocket seemed to pass harmlessly through the rotors, but heavy rounds clapped the armor, or pierced it. The Jolly Green started to pitch and rock. As she climbed away, she was burning. Jack strapped a parachute on his injured man, donned one himself.

When the helicopter exploded, the blast threw Jack out the open door. His parachute opened just above the trees.

Jack's ears were ringing so badly that when the PJ for the other Jolly Green came down to get him, he couldn't hear what the man was saying, could barely hear the thundering of the engines when the second bird hoisted him up, carried him away.

His crewmates were gone, along with the man they'd come for. Quick as that.

When his head cleared, he thought, *I can forgive anything. I can forget anything.*

6. Under the Full Moon

The Willamette has rolled on for few minutes, and Bull hasn't spoken again. But now he says, "The first action I saw was on the night of a full moon." He lets that sentence rest. "We went out on an ambush. The dikes of the rice paddy were slippery. We were careful, trying not to fall down. Quiet."

Bull watches the river, but Jack thinks he must be seeing something else.

"We walked through the village. Eyes on us. I felt them. Now and then, the moon appeared in the rice paddies. The sergeant with the starlight scope said, real soft, 'There!' And he spread us out. These guys were walking right toward us, toward the village, and when the sergeant popped off the first rounds, the rest of us joined in."

Bull falls silent. Jack waits. And goes on waiting until Bull says, "We went forward. Two bodies, and a third guy, shot up, who begged for his life. The sergeant said no dice. He said, 'You.'"

Bull taps his chest. "I did a fucking good job. Had to wrap him like meat to take back. We always had to take them back unless we had the lieutenant. Only officers could confirm. Carrying him back, I felt him watching."

Bull shakes the chain, the dangling cartridge.

"In here. There was mud on my boots from the paddies. I cleaned it off, put it in here. Mud from the place where it happened would keep him from following me, would keep him out of my dreams. And it worked. It worked like a charm. After every ambush, every fire fight, I would scrape a little mud and they couldn't come after me."

7. Names

Jack's father taught him to fish. By the time he was fourteen, Jack had taken Chinook salmon out of the Rogue River and steelhead from the Umpqua; he'd stood hip-deep in the Deschutes, fished the John Day in the shadow of the Umatilla Mountains. Every kid in his class knew where the Columbia was, knew the Willamette flowed through their town, but Jack knew Bully Creek, the Sprague, Crooked River and the Applegate. He could draw them from memory, and he knew how it was to stand in their waters.

Naming the rivers was the first thing. Second was naming the rocks they flowed over: granite, schist, basalt. Then he learned the names of the birds that shared the river with him: osprey, green heron, great blue. He learned the differences between pine and fir, hemlock and spruce, could tell the Scouler willow apart from the Mackenzie willow.

Names were powerful, like incantations. He'd tried using them to weave a spell around Diane Dailey, teaching her, in walks along the river, the names of things she'd grown up never really seeing because she didn't have the names.

Names were so important that when the C-130 flying him to Quang Tri came under fire, the dull dread of his training found its focus: He hadn't been in country for two days, and people were trying to kill him. He was lost. He knew the names of nothing.

On his first mission, standing in the helicopter doorway, he watched rivers pass below. But which rivers? He looked out at the jungle, and the only name he had was *green*.

He knew that he'd never find his way home if he didn't know where he was. He studied the map in the briefing room, learned the shapes and names of the Cam Lo River, the Ia Drang, the Mekong, and the Ma. As for the jungle, no one on base could tell him the names of anything but bamboo. He bought books by mail-order, felt exposed until they came and at last began to learn: *Mangrove. Rubber tree. Banyan. Strangler fig.* He learned the difference between bamboo and Tonkin cane.

Knowing the names was protection. When the cable lowered him into the jungle to find an injured pilot, he'd look on the way down for something he knew the name of: Blackleaf. Scarlet banana. And sometimes he'd see, coiled in the branches and staring at him as if it knew *his* name, a reticulated python.

He would get home.

8. Thunder for Rainfall

Every man who came home different was different in his own way.

Jack traded the thunder of the helicopter's twin engines for the sound of rain rattling a tin roof. It was not so different from where he might have ended up without the war, except that the spruce and pine, the fir and hemlock of home meant more to him now, were more precious. He couldn't live in town or work in town, but needed his solitude. He spent most of his time reading or looking across the vale at a stand of Douglas fir and the crows that glided over. When he needed work, he did odd jobs.

Bull came home hungry, traded the jungle rains for roar of chainsaws. It was not so different from where he might have ended up without the war, except that he was harder now, more aggressive. One summer, he supervised the crews that clear cut that stand of Douglas fir.

9. In a Boat

"It was the monsoon," Bull says. "No way to get anywhere but boat or helicopter, so they sent us up this river in flatbed boats, one squad to a boat. All Charlie needed was patience. The ambush that got us was from both banks of the river. And they had snipers in the trees.

"I tried to get my rifle up, start returning fire like we were supposed to do in an ambush. But I noticed that two guys in my squad were dead, and the thing I kept thinking was, 'Shit. How am I going to get dirt out of a fucking river?' Because it wasn't just the enemy dead. Your own dead would follow you if they could."

Jack waits, then asks, "What did you do?"

"As soon as we were clear, I took off my helmet and dipped it in the river. The corporal in our boat says, 'What the fuck?' But I had it. Muddy water. I didn't need a lot. When the lining dried, I scraped it for a few flakes."

He shakes the cartridge again.

"I kept them here, and they left me alone. For years. For years! But now it's wearing off. I get these headaches. They want me dead. And dead is better than the headaches."

"How do you know it's the ghosts?"

"They tell me. I hear them."

So Jack listens, but hears only the river.

10. Shall We Gather at the River?

Jack met the protestors down by the river because he didn't want to make his speech at the access gate. They'd be too keyed up. He wouldn't have their attention.

"Remember that the loggers aren't our enemies," he said. "Notice what you're carrying in your hearts."

His beard was gray. He was, by now, an elder of the movement and could say these things without seeming naive.

"These men have families. They have children to feed. They think of you as the enemy because this is the only life they know. You may think you see only anger. You may hear only angry words. But they're afraid, and they deserve your compassion. Even if they hate you. Even if they do hateful things."

Then he led them back up the slope, onto the logging road, up to the gate. As they chained themselves by the wrist or by the neck, he pointed out the orange and yellow chanterelles pushing up through the spongy soil in the shadows of the old growth Douglas firs. It was important, he said, to know the names of things.

For a long time there was only the sound of the wind in the treetops.

"Wouldn't it be funny," someone said, "if they just didn't come today?"

But half an hour later, one of Bull Wilson's logging crews arrived, with an escort of state police.

11. With a Gift

Jack watches the river a moment longer. He gets up. He sits closer to Bull. Closer, but still not too close. And he says, "You've got it wrong. You've got it backwards."

Bull looks at him, seems to know for the first time who Jack is.

"The mud and dust you have collected there," Jack says, "it's not protection."

Bull unclenches his fist, draws the cartridge to his palm, considers.

"The ghosts are *in* there," Jack says. "You brought them with you."

Narrowing his eyes, Bull says, "How would *you* know." Now Jack is sure that Bull recognizes him, knows who he is, who he used to be.

"I know," Jack says. "I just do."

Bull loosens his tie. Jack takes that as a good sign, says softly, "Let 'em go."

So Bull Wilson unscrews the container, the hollowed out shell and casing. A few flakes of dust fall.

"Let the river have them," Jack says. He isn't sure he's right. In any case, he doesn't expect any immediate sign. But when Bull throws it all into the Willamette, shell, dust, casing and chain, Jack feels something change in air, as if the river has drawn a breath.

The air gets unstable. Light moves. Jack smells a hint of cordite, of rotten fish, of green decay. Then he can see them, in black pajamas and uniforms of the NVA. In US Army jungle fatigues. The outlines of dead men, the barest hints of memory, standing in the river.

Bull sees them too. Old buddies and old enemies, unreconciled, made of thirty-year-old fear.

No other miracle happens. Jack doesn't expect one, although he feels he is waiting for something. The ghosts are waiting, too.

12. A Woman is a Body of Water

Over the years, the women Jack loved, the women who stayed for longer or shorter times under his tin roof were of a certain sort. They still wore tie dye or granny dresses, strung their own beads. None of them shaved their legs. They ate organic, or vegetarian, or vegan. Some of them said wildly delusional things about Republicans on one hand and witches on the other.

On some nights when such a woman slept beside him, or on other nights when Jack slept alone, Diane would come to him. The Diane of seventeen, of the spring of 1968. But she'd be mixed with the Diane he had sometimes seen with her husband at public hearings, a woman still trim, carefully packaged, running a business of her own. Or so he'd guessed. He never spoke to her. He invented the details he didn't know.

She would come, this Diane who was many Dianes, and offer her breasts to his mouth, the curve of her thighs to his hands. He would stroke himself, feeling the crisp sheets of her bed. Hot summer nights, he would feel the breeze of air conditioning that made her shiver even as his penetrating fingers made her arch and moan.

He would glide into her, filling her, merging the river of his blood with hers.

Wiping the stickiness from his belly with the sheet, he would always feel empowered, relieved, ashamed. The fantasy rooted him in many things he wanted to be free of. Revenge. Old injuries. New enmities. Christ, even air conditioning.

13. Mist

Rain drums so loud on Jack's tin roof that the first sign he has of Diane is the sound of her car door closing. He opens his door before she can knock.

She's wearing blue jeans and a sweater, yellow boots smeared with the mud of his driveway. She has left the car running, lights on, windshield wipers gliding silently from side to side. "Thank you," she says.

"I don't suppose he's altogether whole."

"Who ever is?" Diane laughs. "He's better. He's so much better."

The rain lets up a bit and the wipers begin to squeak. Diane watches his face, and he watches her watching. He wants something, and she seems to know that, but he doesn't have a name for what it is that he wants.

As she says, "If there's anything I can…," Jack says, "It bothers me that…"

She waits. He says, "I know who Bull is. We'll never be friends, but I know who he is." He looks at her, droplets of rain in her hair. "I want to know who you are. Who you have become."

She could take this the wrong way. But she says, "Let's go for a drive."

They follow the rain-slick highway into town. Jack twice thinks he is about to say, *I never stopped wanting you.* He doesn't say it.

"I grow orchids," Diane tells him. "It started as a hobby when the girls were little, but it turned into a business by the time Rae was in high school."

Jack laughs.

"What?" Diane asks.

But he only shakes his head.

She says, "Remember how you tried to impress me with the names of trees?"

"I remember."

Now it's her turn to be silent, to leave him wondering.

There is no sign on the greenhouse. Jack has been by here before, seen the glass roofs, and never imagined that Diane owned them. Inside, the air is hot and moist. Jungle air, but sweeter. Some of the flowers are spotted or striped. One is patterned with gold and rust and white. The ornate petals remind Jack of lace.

"Fascination," she says. "New Moon. Flirtation. Peter Pan." She catches his eye. She is trying not to laugh. "Madonna. Dos Pueblos. Virginia Night. Nikki."

He laughs, and he follows her among the tables, beneath the lights and misting rods, accepting her gift.

Introduction to "Half of the Empire"

The predictability of fairy tales is part of what makes them pleasurable. The hero will pass through travails, often tests that come in threes, to emerge victorious in the end. Even as "Half of the Empire" violates expectations, it fulfills the formula.

Half of the Empire

A young man from a fishing village once went to the Capital to see what he would see. He left his little boat hove up on stony ground beneath the docks, and he gave no thought to the possibility that someone might steal it. He wandered the streets from the fish market to the workshops and foundries, on toward the farm markets and dry markets. The smells of vendors roasting nuts or searing meats made his mouth water, but he had no money. He had only salted fish in his pouch, and after he ate that he was still hungry. Although his stomach growled, he savored the smells more than most men with money would have enjoyed the tastes.

As he went farther and farther from the sea, he marveled at the clothes that grew finer and finer and the manners that were more and more elegant until he scarcely knew his own countrymen. He kept going as the streets widened and led into the hills toward the marvelous white palace, which he stood before and admired for a time. The sun sank low in the sky, and a haze settled over the city. When the young man looked back at the way he had come, he could not see the sea.

As night fell, golden lanterns glowed on the streets. The paper windows of the houses were lit from within. There was no beauty like this in his village, though his village was comfortable enough and had a homely beauty of its own. He had planned to sleep beneath his boat, but with no waves beneath his feet and the stars hidden from view, he had turned so many times that now he had lost his way.

He knocked at a door, thinking that he would ask his way to the docks. He forgot what he meant to say, though, when the woman who answered was the most beautiful he had ever seen. For all her beauty, she looked sad, and her eyes were red as if from crying. Though she appeared to be no older than he was, she met his stare, and when he did not speak she said, "Why have you come?"

The young man said, "To, ah, to see…the master of the house."

"You will regret it," the woman said. She began to weep. "You should turn around and go right back the way you came."

"But I can't," the young man said.

"Because you are so very brave," the woman said. "I know."

"Bravery has nothing to do with it," the young man said. "I'm lost is all."

The woman's weeping ceased. She looked surprised. Indeed, she would have looked no more surprised if the young man had suddenly turned himself into an eel. "No one has ever said that before." Then she frowned. "But you aren't prepared. You're empty handed and perhaps empty headed as well. Are you sure you want to see the master?"

"I am sure."

She led him down a corridor and to a screen. Then she withdrew. As she went away, he could hear her weeping again. "She seems to have sorrows and worries aplenty," the young man said. "I wish I could do something for her." Then he slid the screen aside and stepped into the room behind it.

In the middle of the room sat a giant roasting meat over a brazier. He wore armor and two swords. When he saw the young man, he stood up, unsheathed the longer sword and said, "Why have you come?"

"To see the master of the house. Are you him?"

"I am the master's captain, and to see him, you must come through me. Prepare yourself."

The young man said, "If I have to fight you in order to see the master, I might as well pass the night here instead. It's warm with the brazier burning." The meat sizzled and smoked, and the young man's stomach growled.

"But haven't you come to see the master?"

"To tell you the truth, it's only by chance that I came here. I wanted to see the city, and now that I have seen it, I am ready to go home. But I got lost. When I came to the door, the woman who answered was so beautiful that I forgot what I had meant to say and asked to see the master. That woman is as sad as she is pretty. Do you know why?"

"She weeps for the men who come seeking to claim her. They all die in this room at my sword."

"And have many such men come?"

"Dozens and dozens for years and years."

"I see why she's sad. They must love her very much."

"It's the power they want, for her dowry is half the Empire."

"She's a princess, then?"

"I am surprised that you hadn't heard."

"I'm not from around here," said the young man. "Will you tell me the story?"

The giant lowered his sword. He and the young man sat on either side of the brazier, and the giant told how the princess had been enchanted by the master, who was a powerful sorcerer. She had not aged, but neither had she loved. Several times a year young men from the great cities of the empire came to win her, even though every suitor before them had died.

"She *is* very pretty," the young man said, "but at the moment the thing I am most interested in is getting something to eat and having a warm place to sleep."

"This is quite irregular," said the giant, "but since you didn't really come to fight me, I suppose it would be all right if you stayed as my guest." He drew the shorter sword and used it to cut the meat from the bone, and he gave a portion to the young man. They ate, then sat talking into the night about how to fight with a sword and how to cast a net. "Ah, how this makes me long for my soldiering life," the giant said, "when we would drink wine and talk like brothers, knowing that we might die the next day."

"That's not so different from life in my village," the young man said, "where we drink rice wine by the fire, and the next day one of us may drown." They spoke of wines, then, of which were better, the dry ones of rice or the sweet ones of fruit. The talk of wine made them as drowsy as a drink of wine might have done. At long last, they both fell asleep.

The coals in the brazier burned themselves out. The room grew cold, and the young man woke with the shivers. The giant snored. The cold seemed not to bother him at all. The young man thought that rather than waking the giant, he would see if he could find some more charcoal himself. He slid open the screen to the next room, which was not really a room at all, but a corridor like the one the woman had led him through. At the far end another screen glowed dimly.

"How strange this place is," the young man said to himself. "In my village, we build the rooms of a house next to one another." He walked down the corridor and opened the screen at the other end. The room he stepped into was very large, with wooden shelves lining the walls everywhere except for the place where he had just come in and a screen on the other side. Books and scrolls were stacked on the shelves, and they rose toward a ceiling so high that the young man couldn't see it in the darkness. The books might have gone up forever.

In the center of the room was a table where a bald man with a long white beard sat reading by the light of a candle. The young man crossed the room, and stood before the table. The white-haired man did not look up. He rubbed his temples as he read.

"Are you the master?" the young man said.

The old man looked up with a start. "You're here!" he said. "No one has ever come this far!" He patted himself as if to see if he were dreaming. "The master? No, I'm not the master. I'm his librarian, and I hadn't expected you. I haven't read quite all of them yet."

"I'd like some charcoal. The brazier has gone out," the young man explained.

"Brazier? That's of no importance. You've come to the library seeking the secret of the maze. Let me see, now. Which riddle shall I ask you?" He carried the candle to one of the shelves and squinted as he held the flame close to the bindings. He groaned. "The ink fades every year. It gets harder and harder to read these."

"Perhaps the brazier doesn't matter to you," the young man said, "but I'm quite cold sleeping in the other room."

"Pay no attention to the cold," the librarian said. "If you're to see the master, it's the mind that matters. What a man wants is knowledge and a sharp wit."

"What I want is fuel," the young man said. "Or a blanket."

The librarian was about to take a scroll from the shelf, then stopped and looked at the young man. "From the provinces. Ho! I know the one. You'll never get it." He crossed the room and selected a book. The binding was tied closed, and the old man was some time plucking at the string with his fingernails. At last he loosened the knot and opened the book. He squinted at the page, rubbing his temples again. "How my head aches. If only the candle burned a little brighter."

"I don't mind riddles," the young man said, "but what I really want…"

"Solve the riddle and you'll see the master," said the librarian, "and the master will give you your heart's desire. Now listen." He bent very close to the page until his nose almost touched. "The marks are so very faint. Hardly there at all. 'I proceed until I am no more, but there I am behind me once again.'"

The young man thought a moment and said, "A wave."

"No!" the librarian said. "It's the Emperor."

"Are you sure?" the young man said. "Is that what's in the book?"

The librarian looked at the page again. "To tell the truth, I can't make it out, but I am sure I remember this one. It's the Emperor."

"But a wave is just as good an answer. Where I come from, it's a better answer because we see waves every day, but we've never seen the Emperor."

The librarian frowned. "I picked this one because of course you haven't seen the Emperor. It's supposed to be hard." He stroked his beard. "But I suppose you are right. Not all wit or learning are already in books. Some of it still needs thinking up and writing down. I could write in the character for 'wave,' and then that would be the right answer and I could tell you how to pass the maze." And that is what he did.

The young man opened the screen and went through the branching corridors according to the librarian's directions. The corridors branched and turned, turned and branched. The young man came at last to another screen. He opened it, and there in the center of a large room, a brazier burned with a yellow flame. Next to the brazier was a pile of charcoal. A great heap of treasure gleamed in the firelight. There were rings and swords, a robe suitable for an Emperor, coins and pearls, boxes of jewels. There were other, more common things as well: a lamp, a mirror, a silken kerchief and a jar of wine.

The flame grew brighter, and a voice from within it spoke and said, "Take what you will."

The young man filled a sack with charcoal. Then he took up the lamp, the kerchief and the wine. To the flame he said, "How do I find my way to the docks beside the fish market?"

The flame told him the way to take. Then the young man retraced his steps. He left the lamp with the librarian, who lit it and found that it burned very bright indeed. How it would relieve his aching head! In the captain's room, the young man rekindled the brazier and slept near it until morning. He made a gift of wine to the giant, who was as pleased as he was amazed. At the front door of the house, the young man met the woman and gave her the silken kerchief, saying, "Dry your tears. Not every story here is a sad one. I have seen the master, and I did not die in the attempt." Then he made to leave.

"But if you have seen the master," the woman said, "then you have become a great lord and half the Empire is yours." She knelt. "If what you say is true, then I am to be your bride and Empress."

"I have never seen a woman more beautiful," said the young man, "but I am not a man of the Capital or any city. My life is on the sea. It is a hard life that would not suit you."

He left her. He followed the directions that the master of the house had given him. He recovered his little boat from beneath the dock, and he sailed home to his village. In time, he married a girl who had grown up nearby and they had children. In time, they grew old and had grandchildren. In time, they died.

Some say that the young man was a fool to turn down half the Empire.

Others say that if a mere fisherman had taken half the Empire, the other half would have gone to war against his rule and he would have come to ruin.

And a very few say that he had already possessed half the Empire before this story began, and that what he had refused was the *other* half. But the few who say this are strange. Very strange.

Introduction to "Whalesong"

I get a lot of my writing ideas in the shower, enough that I sometimes keep a grease pencil alongside the shampoo so that I can take notes on the glass shower door. "Whalesong," the earliest story in this collection, was a shower story. The inspiration came when I was living in a roach-infested studio apartment that had musical plumbing. One day as I rinsed, the pipes sang to me: *Arooooo-ank. Skeeeeeee. Thunk tunk tunk.* My hair was still wet as I started to write.

Whalesong

"I don't know why you expect me to get all weepy about it, Mother," Helen said into the phone. "It's not like David and I had an ideal marriage."

"Helen," her mother said, "the man is dead."

"And I'm sorry, just like I'd be sorry for any other stranger dying on the highway." From the hallway bathroom cane a high-pitched *Skyreeee? Skyreeee?* and then a *Thunk-thunk-thunk-thunk-thunk.* Helen covered the receiver.

"Richard!" she called out. "What are you doing?"

"Nothing!"

"Well cut out whatever's making the funny noise."

"It's not me, Mom."

Helen uncovered the receiver. "Sorry. Richard was making some noise in the bathroom."

Her mother's voice said, "How are the kids taking it?"

"Pretty well. They cry some, and then they're O.K. We're all handling it like troopers."

"Helen, that's not natural."

"Oh, come on, Mother. He wasn't around much for them, either. It's hard to miss someone you hardly see."

"Listen to me," said her mother. "You're being awfully stony about this. You sound a lot like your father, just too reasonable and hard to be believed. And that's what finally killed him, you know."

"A heart attack is what killed him."

"Helen, I'm telling you, no matter how far apart you and David were, he was your husband for twelve years. You lived under the same roof…"

"Technically, yes. Like tenants in the same building."

"What I'm saying," Helen's mother said, "is that it's not natural for you not to grieve even a little."

From the bathroom came *Skyreeee? Skyreeee?*, followed by a low, vibrating *Ooooooooooomp*.

"Richard, cut it out!"

"I'm just washing my hands."

"Mother, I've got to go," Helen said, and hung up. Then, marching down the hall, she said, "Young man, when I'm on the phone I expect a little—"

"It wasn't me!" Richard said as she entered the bathroom. "The pipes make noise when the water runs." He turned the faucet, and as the water ran, the bathroom filled with *Skyreeee? Skyreeee?* and then *Thunk-thunk-thunk-thunk*. "See?"

"O.K.," Helen said. "Not guilty. Where's your sister?"

"I don't know."

"Well, find her and get her to set the table, and you pour drinks. I want water."

"Can I have Coke?"

"No, you cannot have Coke. You and Carissa can drink milk like you always do with dinner, and I wish you would stop asking. Now, go get your sister."

Richard's shoulders slumped as though some of his bones had suddenly vanished, and he sighed, "O.K."

"Don't you drag your feet," Helen said. "Scoot."

When Richard filled his mother's glass at the kitchen sink, the pipes said *Aaaawooooot*, and then echoed *Ootootoot*.

"God, that's irritating," Helen said as she pulled the casserole from the oven.

"The toilet does it, too," said Carissa. "And the bathroom sink." She drummed on the table with two spoons.

"Do you want to go to your room?" Helen asked.

"No," Carissa said, still drumming.

"Then cool it and finish setting the table."

Helen had always been amazed at how long the kids could dawdle over loading the dishwasher. Tonight, after trying unsuccessfully to read the newspaper in the living room while they fought and carried one glass or one fork at a time from the table, she sent them to bed early and finished the job herself. When she turned the appliance on, it sang a rising and falling *Aaaa-ank. Aaaaaa-ank. Aaaaaaaaaa-aaaaank.*

"All right," she said. "That's enough!"

In the garage she opened David's toolbox, and as she touched the cool metal of the tools, she felt a tremor move from her hand and into her arm. She closed her eyes and said deliberately, "I will need a locking pliers and a pipe wrench and maybe a screwdriver," though she actually had little idea what she might need or what she might do with it.

Inside the house again, she heard Carissa calling her.

"What is it?" Helen said from the hall.

Long silence.

"What!"

"I want a drink of water."

"You're a big girl. You get a drink yourself, and then you get right back in bed. No dillydallying." She turned and walked toward the stairwell.

"Mom?"

"What now?"

Another long silence.

"Carissa, what?"

Again, silence, and Helen turned toward the basement stairs.

As she started down, she felt strange, as though her limbs grew a little heavier with each step. The air felt thickened. Down. Down. Each step took longer than the one before it. Down. She became aware of the effort required to fill her lungs. There was a distant roaring sound, like the surf heard from afar. Each breath slow. Each step deliberate. From the bottom of the stairs, the light bulb at the top of the stairwell looked far away and shimmery. The basement air was damp. Helen put her forearm against the cold wall and took a long, slow breath. Just breathing in and breathing out was hard work.

Far away, she heard Carissa call, "Mom?" but she turned toward the rec room, heading toward the utility room beyond. Slow steps. Now, though, she no longer felt heavy. Instead, it was as though she were no heavier than the air, and she had to move slowly because with each step she had to concentrate on keeping her feet on the floor. She switched on the blue light over the pool table, and it seemed dimmer and bluer than she remembered it. Her hand felt the switch on the utility room wall, but no light came when she made it click several times with a hollow sound. She swam into the room with the murky blue light behind her.

The room stretched out farther in front of her than reason told her it could. She couldn't see the walls. Two black immensities floated like zeppelins in the space in front of her, one a little larger than the other. Far away, as though through many walls of glass, she heard Carissa's feet on the floor above her. Whales, she saw in the dim light. They were whales. And when Carissa turned the faucet upstairs and the water began to flow in the pipes, the whales slowly turned their bodies toward the familiar sound, and the larger one cried, *Skyreeee? Aaaaaaa-ank.*

The smaller one answered, *Aaaaaa-ank. Thunk-thunk-thunk-thunk.* Then the water in the pipes stopped.

Helen looked at the tools in her hands. The metal was warm. She thought of David's hands on them, and then of her own hands in David's. Large hands, she remembered. When had he last held her hands in his, sheltering them, nesting them? So very long ago. How far she and David had drifted. Distantly, she heard Carissa returning to bed. Helen turned and started slowly away. She switched off the blue light. Slow, difficult steps. At the bottom of the stairs, she felt for a moment that she would float away on a black current, back into the darkness. But then she mounted the first step and felt a little better with each subsequent progression toward the yellow light and the air.

She woke before dawn, and started the coffee brewing. In her bathroom she saw David's tools lying on the counter. She picked up the screwdriver, and it felt hard and cold in her hand. She made herself laugh a short, uncertain laugh. Whales.

She stepped into the shower, and as the water began to fall, she heard *Skyreeee? Skyreeee?* and an answering *Awoooooot. Thunk-thunk-thunk-thunk.* This time she couldn't make herself laugh. Instead she heard a sound come from inside her like air escaping, reluctantly, from a balloon. *Eeeeeee.* Short breath. *Eeeeeeee.* And then she managed a sob, and she began to add her own song to the song of the whales. She sang for the seas, for the ancient seas that surrounded us once, that carried our voices across such distances that no matter how far we drifted, we were never alone.

Introduction to "How Golf Shaped Scotland"

I am a terrible golfer. It's hard to say whether I spend more on greens fees or lost balls. As bad as I am, though, I enjoy what amounts to a long walk over sculpted terrain. In fact, when I shank another ball out of bounds or into the water, it's comforting to just stand for a while admiring the landscape, as if I weren't playing some stupid game at all.

How Golf Shaped Scotland

Some say that the town of St. Andrews in Scotland is the cradle of golf. That much is true. Some also say that the rolling land thereabouts was made for golf, and that is surely wrong. Those sandy hillocks, the links of St. Andrews, were not made *for* golf, but rather *by* golf.

Long ago, when the fairy folk of Scotland were seen more often, a priest called Father Iain lived in a village not far from where St. Andrews is today. Father Iain was the son and grandson of great swordsmen. He had a warrior's strong arm, and his eyes were as sharp as the finest archer's. But he never wielded sword nor bow, and the only club he ever held was a slender rod of hazelwood attached to a thick applewood head. A golf club.

More precisely, the only club Father Iain ever held was a putter, for at that time, a putter was the only sort of golf club there was and the ball was a round white stone. The very shape of Scotland was different, too. In those days, the margin along the coast was flat. Sheep cropped the grass so close that the land was like green felt laid upon a table top. Few men played golf in those days, first because there were always wars to fight against the English, and second because the game was so boring. One hole was the same as the last, and one course of the flat ground was akin to any other.

But even a boring game was at least something. After all, a man like Father Iain—a man with a warrior's strong arm and eyes as sharp as the finest archer's—cannot be ever and always indoors, even if he is a man of peace. Father Iain played often, putting the white stone from this hole to that, and he played well. He often wished for something more, however. A man of his abilities wants a challenge, and golf gave him but a little of that.

None of the villagers who bothered to try could beat Father Iain. Theirs was a small village and poor. They had little to be proud of. Is it any wonder then, that the villagers bragged about their golfing priest? "Aye, Father Iain's the best," they boasted to any who would listen. "There is no finer player on this earth nor in it."

That was bragging indeed, for while mortal man lives *on* the earth, the wee folk live *in* it. The boulders are their homes. The great halls of their clans and kingdoms lie beneath the ground.

Father Iain knew that he was good with his putter, but he also knew not to tempt the powers of the Earth. "Be careful what ye say," the priest cautioned his flock. "Do not seem to challenge the wee folk on my behalf."

Well, it was as true then as it is now that when a priest says not to do something there are those who cannot resist doing it for that reason alone. The villagers began to say to one another, "To be sure, our Father Iain could even beat the fair folk at this game!"

Never let it be said that the fairies do not like a challenge. One moonlit night, when all the village slept, someone rapped insistently on Father Iain's door. When the priest opened wide the door, who did he behold but a wee little man and a wee little woman, both of them dressed in finery and each holding a gnarled stick and a white stone.

"It's a cauld night the night," Father Iain observed and added politely, "Will ye come in by the fire, strangers?"

"Thank ye, no. We are the King and Queen of Faery," said the King. "We've come to take up your challenge."

"Challenge? I made no challenge!"

"Play us, mortal man," said the Queen, "and if ye win, ye shall indeed be the champion golfer of Scotland."

"That is of no import to me," said Father Iain.

"And we shall lift the curse," said the King.

"The curse?" said Father Iain. "What curse?"

"Why, the curse we have just now laid," said the Queen. "That every cow in the village should go dry and every hen cease laying, that every sheep grow sickly and every bit of man-tilled ground go barren."

"Ye must play and beat us both for us to lift the spell," said the King, and he named a time and place three nights hence for the contest.

In the morning, Father Iain slept later than he meant to, and when he awoke, he had to hurry to prepare for the mass. As he bustled about, he thought that the King and Queen's visit must have been a dream.

When he got to the kirkyard, though, he found his parishioners waiting for him and looking worried.

"Good Father," said one of the women, "my little bairns are lowing for a sup o' milk, but their mothers have none to give!"

"My hens have not laid today," said a man.

"D'ye ken sich a prayer as will lift a curse?" asked another, "for sure it is that cursed we are."

"Let us celebrate the mass and see what prayers can be said," Father Iain told them. But though the villagers followed him in for the mass that morning, and though they gathered the next morning and the next in the pews of the kirk, their prayers did not deliver them. For three days, the cows gave no milk, the hens did not lay, all the sheep trembled with some sickness. Even the turnip leaves began turning brown. Only then did Father Iain tell his parish of the curse that the fair folk had laid.

"To be sure," said he, "these are the wages of boasting, and God will not deliver us from a curse we have earned." He might have said, *a curse that* ye *have earned*, but he was a kinder and holier man than that.

Father Iain had no choice but to take up his putter on the appointed night and walk out upon the sward to meet the little King and Queen by moonlight.

Now anyone who has heard aught of the wee folk knows that they love to win by trickery. Father Iain did not expect fair play, and sure enough, when they all approached the first hole, the priest found that a little hillock stood between his ball and the hole. In a place so flat as Scotland was in those days, such a feature was rare.

"Strange," said Father Iain. "I do not recall any mound of earth here, and I have played these same holes often."

"There's many a strange thing in the world," said the Queen of Faery with a smile. She and the King putted out. Father Iain putted over the hillock as best he could, but he fell a stroke behind.

When they all approached the second hole, they saw that this time a little hillock stood between the Queen's ball and the hole.

"How very odd," the Queen said, looking at her husband. "I know this ground like I know my own mind, and yet I find a mound here where I'm sure none was before."

"There's many an odd thing in the world," the King of Faery said with a smile.

The Queen gave him a glare that would have set a stick on fire, but the King took no notice. Father Iain and the King of Faery putted out in one stroke, but the Queen lost a stroke getting over the hillock.

Father Iain knew now that he had a chance. "It may be that I cannot win and lift the curse," he said aloud, "for though the Queen is no better than I, the King is a stroke ahead. Clearly he is the better golfer."

But at the third hole, the King's ball rolled into a patch of sand that he swore had not existed before he hit his ball, and then all three were tied.

The rest of the game, for nine holes out and nine holes back, continued in this way. The King and Queen used their powers against each other as much as against Father Iain. They took turns pulling a stroke ahead, and then falling a stroke behind. As the three players putted close to the final hole—which was the hole they had started with—all were tied again.

When the King took his turn, the ground rippled and turned his ball aside. He glared at the Queen.

Then it was her turn. She hit her ball right toward the hole, but again the ground shook and shifted, forming a little gutter that drew her ball away. She glared at the King.

Now it was the priest's turn. His ball was only as far from the hole as a man is tall.

The Queen of Faery said to the King, "However this game falls out between us, we mustn't let this mortal man win!"

And the King said, "Agreed."

What hope could the priest have now of lifting the curse? The King and Queen of the very Earth were united against him. The ground he must putt across would ripple and roll, dip and rise, and carry his ball astray.

But Father Iain had a warrior's strong arm and eyes as sharp as the finest archer's. He had a warrior's wit, as well, and saw the path his ball must take. By the light of the moon, he found a sharp stone, and he split the head of his putter at an angle so that the bottom was thicker than the top, like a wedge.

"Hit the ball," said the King, "or we will be at this all night!"

"As ye wish," said Father Iain. And though the powers of Faery were united against Father Iain, though the earth bubbled and wiggled like a pot of boiling porridge, he hit the ball with his damaged putter, which was a putter no longer, but the very first niblick ever made. And no Earthly powers could do aught to alter its course, for the ball went not along the ground, but through the air, and did not meet the earth until it struck the bottom of the hole.

"This would not have happened if ye'd played better!" said the King of Faery to his Queen.

"It would not have happened if *ye* had played better!" she answered.

"And what of the curse?" said Father Iain. "Is it lifted?"

If the King and Queen heard him at all, they gave no sign. Glowering at one another, they turned their backs on Father Iain and began to play again. As they played through the night, they made the earth hump and drop all the more. Dunes great and small rose up. Brooks and burns flowed where none had flowed before, and pools and mires appeared.

In the morning, the villagers were astonished to see how the shape of the land had changed. Over the weeks and months that followed, the land everywhere along the sea changed from flat to rolling. Where before the ground had been level, now there were dunes and hillocks everywhere.

As for Father Iain, he was much relieved to find that the village cows again gave milk, the hens once more laid, the flocks regained their health, and the meager gardens yielded as much as they ever had.

What's more, he found the game of golf was much improved by the altered landscape and by the addition of a few new clubs that lifted the ball into the air.

It would be many years yet before golf was played with a leather ball stuffed with feathers, but it was now a game that could truly hold a man's attention, even a man with a warrior's strong arm and eyes as sharp as the finest archer's. No one could ever match Father Iain, though he played the game till the very end of his days.

Introduction to "In the Chief's Name"

Eugene, Oregon, where I live, is famous for its anarchists. At the World Trade summit in Seattle, much of the vandalism may have been the work of Eugene's band of black-clad saboteurs. Eugene anarchists were convicted of torching several SUVs on a local car dealer's lot. On a smaller scale, Eugene anarchists employed a vandalism campaign to drive one of my favorite restaurants out of business for fear that a popular, trendy success in their low-rent neighborhood would result in the gentrification of the district. Sooner or later, I had to write about these people.

The story is also about Chief Seattle, who never made the beautiful speech that is attributed to him, the speech about the decline of his way of life and the rise of the white man. Indeed, there are multiple texts for a speech that Seattle supposedly made, but each one of them was written by white men who were inventing their own versions of what they wanted the chief to be and say, for their own political purposes. I've done the same thing again, putting words in his mouth. At least I'm telling you up front that this is fiction.

In the Chief's Name

Rain pattered on the metal roof of the van. Wolf sat on the carpet scraps in back with his eyes closed, listening, waiting for Peach and Raven to finish setting up the antenna. He opened his eyes when the back door of the van jerked open. As Peach and Raven piled in, Wolf could see the lighted second-story windows of the houses on either side of the alley. Inside the van, he could see the jumble of radio gear and tools on the floor, the tangle of wires. The door shut. It was darker than ever.

"All set," Raven said. He dropped something. It sounded like the vice grips. "You ready?"

Wolf clicked on a dim red bulb overhead. He checked his meters and put on his headphones. "Here we go."

Peach put on her own headphones and leaned close to Wolf. She smelled of wet hair and patchouli oil. "Gonna play the loop?"

"Of course, baby." The loop had been her idea. She'd heard something like it while listening to short-wave radio. It was supposed to help listeners find the station they were looking for, although in this case, it was just window dressing. The broadcast signal from the van wouldn't even carry across Lake

Washington to Bellevue most nights, and the broadcast schedule was necessarily irregular.

Wolf started the loop. Over his headphones he heard the hoot of an owl, then a howling wolf, and finally his own recorded voice: "This is Radio Free Seattle, FM." After a beat, it repeated. He could also hear the signal of the commercial radio station whose signal they were treading on just enough to pull listeners away from it.

Raven's hands were cupped over his own earphones. "Sounds good, man. This was a good idea, Peach."

Wolf gave Raven a glance that he meant as a warning, but the red light was dim enough that expressions were hard to read. He couldn't tell if Raven got the message.

"I mean it," Raven said. He put his hand on Peach's shoulder. "It sounds totally professional."

Wolf snorted. "Oh, great. We sound totally professional. We can all get jobs doing this. We can all have careers."

Peach ignored that and said to Raven, "Thanks."

Wolf grabbed his mike and flipped two switches. Peach said, "Hey, let the loop run for a while. The idea is supposed to be—"

"This is Radio Free Seattle, broadcasting tonight on eighty-nine point seven. Wake up, sleepy heads! It's time to change the world. Radio Free Seattle is here to tell you how. Tonight, we'll be giving the city some of the medicine it needs."

"That's right, we're here to..." Raven started to say. His mike was dead. In the darkness, Wolf suppressed a smile.

"We're here to tell you about direct action," Peach said into her microphone, "the kind of action we're taking ourselves, tonight, to take back the earth from the corporations."

"And what exactly are we going to do?" Wolf said.

"We're going to kill machines," Peach answered. "We're going to monkey-wrench one small corner of the Evil Empire."

"You're so right, honey," Wolf said. "Come Monday morning, when the corporations start up their machines, at least one company is going to be in for a nasty surprise."

Raven had found the end of his mike cord. "This was plugged in when I left the van," he said to Wolf.

"Shit happens," Wolf said over the air. "But it doesn't happen nearly enough yet. It's going to take more than the efforts of Radio Free Seattle to shut down the machineries of enslavement. That's where you come in, citizens. We're on the air to urge you to join us."

Raven plugged himself in. "That's right…" His mike was still dead.

"Now maybe you're saying to yourself, 'Who are these criminals, and why in the world do they think I'd want to join them?' Well, we're just human beings who don't want to be slaves. We're the resistance."

"In case you haven't noticed," said Peach, "our way of life sucks."

"Citizens, wake up! The air is foul. The water is poisoned. Concrete creeps foot by foot over the whole world."

"Cities suck," said Peach.

Raven flipped a switch. "Yeah," he said, but his mike still wasn't working.

"We're on our way to logging the last virgin forest. We're raping the earth with our mines."

"Mining sucks," said Peach.

"Some say it's time to go back to the earth, but before long, there isn't going to be any earth to go back to. We can't see our mother earth any more. We're blinded by money."

"Money sucks," said Peach. "So does farming."

"Citizen, the average hunter-gatherer spends three hours a day getting food and shelter. The rest of his time is his own. How does that sound to you, Mr. Suit-and-Tie? How'd you like to have everything you really need with three hours of work a day, Ms. Cell-Phone?"

Raven reached for a switch in front of Wolf. Wolf swatted his hand away.

"Asshole," Raven said.

"The thing the corporations don't want you to know," Wolf said, "is how vulnerable they are. If technological society falls apart, if it all breaks down, then it can't possibly be started up again. All the easy metals have been mined already. All the easy oil has been pumped. If we stepped back to an earlier time for just a little while, the poisonous technologies and the enslaving corporations would suffer a blow that they could not ever recover from. Are you a happy slave, citizen? You have the power to be free!"

"Every machine that breaks down is a step in the right direction," said Peach.

"A different life is possible," Wolf said. "Break the machines, stop the corporations, and we can start from scratch. How will we do it? We'll do it as free humans have always done. We'll make it up as we go along."

"Don't give in!" Peach said.

"Some people say to me, 'Man, don't you realize that what you're doing is criminal?' Hey, I'll tell you what a crime is. A crime is making people slaves while your advertising convinces them they are free. Most of you don't even see how far it's gone, how powerless you are until you resist."

Peach said, "So resist!"

Wolf opened a book to a page he had marked. He squinted in the dim light to read. "In the words of Chief Seattle, the Suquamish Indian whose lands were stolen to make this city, 'The dogs of appetite will devour the rich earth and leave only desert.' Chief Seattle saw what we were headed for. Money and technology aren't the answer. Their time is passing. No more machines. Earth and stone, muscle and bone. That's the world we're talking about. That's anarchy. That's freedom. And that's the future. We go out tonight to do battle. We go out in Chief Seattle's name. Long live freedom!"

Raven leaned close enough to Peach's microphone that his voice chimed in with hers when they both said, "Long live freedom!"

"This is Radio Free Seattle. Good night." Wolf shut the transmitter off. "Okay. Take the antenna down and let's get moving."

"You take it down, jerk wad," Raven said.

Wolf looked at him. "What's your problem?"

"You *are* being a jerk," Peach said. "We're all in this together."

"What in the world are you talking about? The microphone? We were in the middle of a broadcast! I can't have Raven fiddling with stuff when we're on the air!"

"You really are unbelievable sometimes," Raven said.

"You're cranky because you didn't get to talk on the radio?" Wolf said. "And I'm the jerk?"

"Yes! You act like…" Raven looked at Peach, then he looked at the floor of the van. "Just forget it," he said.

"No. Say it. I act like what?"

Raven picked his tools up off the floor. "Light."

Wolf just looked at him.

"Peach," said Raven, "kill the light."

Wolf switched off the red light. Raven opened the door and jumped out.

"Remember. You don't own me," Peach said. Then she followed Raven into the rain.

Wolf slapped the side of the pre-amp with his palm.

When they set up again further north, close to Carkeek Park, Wolf made a show of double-checking Raven's microphone before they went on the air. They broadcast pretty much the same message. Raven didn't say much. He was sulking.

This time Wolf read at length from Chief Seattle's famous speech to the white invaders. Wolf invoked Seattle's name at the end of the broadcast. He did this again during their third broadcast from a location way down south, toward Renton. By the time they packed up for the last time and headed for the construction site, Raven seemed to have finished sulking.

"That Indian stuff is good," he told Wolf.

"The dude was righteous," Wolf agreed.

Wolf parked the van two blocks away. Then the three of them made a walking reconnaissance without any gear, just to check things out. The site looked the same as it had on other nights: a pit two stories deep, no security lights. There was a trailer down there with a light on, but they hadn't seen any sign of a night watchman. Two trucks. Four big earth movers. A couple of compressors. Plenty of targets.

Traffic was rare at three in the morning. Maybe half a dozen cars went by during their whole reconnaissance.

Back at the van, they put on the radio headsets, then covered them with hats so that only the little microphones showed, and those were subtle. Wolf put on black gloves. He slung one of the packs onto his shoulder. Raven took the other. At the site, Raven helped Wolf over the fence and dropped the packs down to him.

"Sound check," Wolf said as he walked down the grade into the pit.

"Check," came Raven's voice in his ear. Then Peach: "Check."

At the bottom of the pit, Wolf kept to the shadows and waited until Peach and Raven told him they were in position, that there were no cars or pedestrians that might spot him.

"Okay," Wolf said. "Keep an eye on that trailer, too. Just in case."

He went for the big machines first. Climbing onto the bulldozer, he found and unscrewed the crankcase lid. From one of the packs, he took a caulk gun that was loaded with the mixture they had made at Raven's apartment: oil-based grinding compound and salt. Wolf said, "In Chief Seattle's name," then injected the whole tube into the dozer's crankcase. On

Monday, when the workers started the dozer up, the engine would do the work of grinding itself into junk.

The hair stood up on Wolf's neck even before Peach said, "Car." Wolf crouched in the shadows of the bulldozer and watched the lights sweep by on Madison.

"Okay," Peach said.

Wolf still had the creeps. Someone was watching.

"You sure?" he said.

A pause. "Yeah. You're clear."

"Is *everybody* sure?" They didn't use names on the radio, not for their broadcasts, and not for their direct actions.

"You're clear," said Raven.

Wolf still didn't move. "I got a bad feeling."

"Nothing on the street, nothing in the trailer," said Peach.

"Quit being paranoid," Raven said. "You're clear."

Wolf slowly looked over the construction site. Nothing moved. "Okay," he said. He went to the next bit of heavy machinery. "In Seattle's name," he said softly as he monkey-wrenched the crankcase. And he had the same feeling again that he was being watched, that he was being betrayed.

Paranoid, Raven had called him. Well, what if it turned out that he had good reason to be paranoid? Maybe it wasn't some stranger who was creeping him out. Maybe it was Raven. Or Raven and Peach together. If they were messing around behind his back...

Would they turn on him? No, not Peach. Not his Peachy girl. Even if she were going to turn him out, she wouldn't do it this way. Raven, then.

Wolf opened the hood of the first truck. An engine this size only needed half a dose of corundum and salt. Chief Seattle had said that the white man lived like a snake eating its own tail, and the tail was getting shorter and shorter. This was like feeding shards of glass into the maw of the corporate snake. Wolf smiled. "Die, snake!" he said.

"What?" Raven said.

"Car," said Peach.

Wolf hopped down.

"It's a cop car," Peach said. "I don't think he can see you from that lane. Be cool."

Wolf felt his heart beating.

"On my side, now," said Raven. "He's slowing."

"Shit." Peach said. For a moment, that was all. Then, "Two more on my side."

"Tuck your mikes under your hats," Wolf said as he grabbed both packs and ran back to the bulldozer. "Walk away. They can stop you. They can talk to you." He tripped, got up. "But they can't make you show ID. They can't arrest you for taking a walk on a public sidewalk." He threw the packs between the dozer treads and crawled in after them. A car door slammed. A moment later, a powerful flashlight beam swept over the ground.

Wolf tried willing them to go away. *There's nothing here*, he thought. *The lock's still on the gate. Nothing's amiss. False alarm.*

Another flashlight beam joined the first. He heard the voices of police radios.

"They're talking to her," said Raven's voice.

"Shut up," Wolf said softly. "What if they're listening?"

"If someone's listening in, then we're screwed anyway, aren't we?" said Raven. "She's cool. I can tell just looking that she's cool."

"Where are you?"

"I'm in an alley. They can't see me."

"They've got lights, asshole."

"Oh, so I'm an asshole for wanting to keep an eye on her?"

"Just keep walking. Get out of here."

"She's waving goodbye and walking away. Told you she's cool. I'll go parallel, make sure she gets back without a hassle. Sit tight, man. Maybe they'll pack up and go away."

"How did they know?"

"Tall buildings. Lots of windows. Maybe some janitor called it in."

"On the weekend? No way, you bastard."

Wolf couldn't see the flashlight beams any longer, but he could still hear the police radios up above.

"What are you saying?" Raven said, but his signal was weak.

"What I'm saying, asshole, is that I'm not so sure you want me around. If my ass is in jail, you've got Peach all to yourself."

"No names," said Peach. "You are totally losing your cool."

"You okay, baby?"

"I'm fine. Don't do anything stupid." Her signal, like Raven's, was thready.

"You neither," he said. He heard another car arrive, something with a rough idle. He ventured a peek. Headlights shone on a section of the fence above. Somebody was unlocking and unchaining the gate. "Shit."

After the police dog had found him, after it was already too late because the cops had their flashlights on him, that's when he thought about his radio. What he should have done, while he still had time, was strip the thing off and feed it into the tread wheels. Or bury it. Anything to get rid of the evidence that he hadn't acted alone. They hauled him out and read him his rights, which he already knew: He didn't have to talk to them. He didn't have to answer any questions. He could even make them stop asking, "Who was on the other end? Who were you talking to?" All he had to do was say he wanted his lawyer present, and they had to shut up.

He'd been over the procedures a hundred times with Peach and Raven. Get caught alone, take the punishment alone. The important thing was the movement. Even if one of them got sentenced to some prison time, the important thing was to keep someone on the outside doing the work that needed to be done, shutting it all down.

Now, however, he couldn't stop thinking about Peach and Raven. Even if Raven were innocent of any betrayal, which Wolf heartily doubted, there they'd be, the two of them. Peach would need comforting. Raven would know just what to do, just how to console her and take her mind off of poor old Wolf, sitting in some cell. There, there, Peachy baby. There, there.

So he gave them up. Legal names. Addresses. The garage where they kept a drum of valve grinding compound. It all went so fast that it was still dark outside when the cops finally moved him to a holding cell.

It must have been a slow night. There was one other guy in the cell, and he was asleep, face to the wall, snoring. Wolf sat down on the opposite side of the cell, on the edge of the shelf that served as a bed.

He put his face in his hands. He was a jerk. He was an asshole. He was every name he could think of. Where was his commitment? After all that planning, he had caved right in and given it all up. Now they were all screwed. One stupid night of jealousy, and he had pissed it all away.

"It's better this way," said a voice from right beside him.

Wolf started. There was someone sitting right next to him. Someone who hadn't been there a moment before. A man wearing a conical hat.

Wolf's heart pounded in his throat. "Who…?" He stood up and backed away.

The man's hat was dripping. Water puddled at his bare feet. Around his shoulders he wore a blanket and a sort of cape made of woven reeds. His face looked weathered, dark.

"When you keep speaking the name of a dead person, you hold him or her to this world. The Bostons didn't understand that. The Bostons didn't understand lots of things." He frowned.

"Bostons?"

"Your people. The white people."

"I don't..." Wolf's head felt light.

"Better sit down."

Wolf sat. "S-Seattle?"

"Close enough." The Indian frowned. "Even if they don't ever say my name right, it's close enough to hold me here." He pulled the cape and blanket closer. "I should be far away by now. But your people had the bad manners to give my name to this place."

"I don't know what to...I'm sorry." Wolf rubbed his forehead. "This can't be happening."

"Life is like that. Death, too. Things that can't be happening happen all the time." He pursed his lips. "It's going to take a long time for me to leave this place now. It's going to take a long time for people to stop speaking my name."

"Seattle. Chief Seattle. I..." Wolf stood up. He sat back down. "Seattle! It's an honor!"

"Mmm." The ghost frowned.

"Oh, your name. I'm sorry. It's just...I admire your words."

"No you don't. Not *my* words. But all night you were saying my name and sticking it onto words that someone else said. That was the first thing that made me mad."

"'Continuing to contaminate his own bed, the white man will one night suffocate in his own filth,'" Wolf quoted from memory. "Didn't you say that?"

"No! Some poet said that and mixed my name up in it. Ever since I died, this has been going on. Every time white people change their ideas about what they want Indians to be, someone makes a new speech for me."

Wolf swallowed. "But..." He rubbed his head. Could he really be having this conversation? "But we're trying to take back the land. Maybe the words aren't exactly what you said, but what my friends and I want is a return to the old ways. Your ways."

"My ways? You don't know anything about my ways."

"I mean your people. Living off the land."

"Mmm." Another frown.

"See, the world is going to turn back to simpler ways of doing things. It *has* to. We don't need bulldozers and skyscrapers to be happy!"

"Those digging machines are pretty good for digging."

"We have our hands. We can make stone tools."

Seattle grunted dismissively. "I remember my first iron ax. Now that could cut!"

"Okay, but iron comes out of mines and mines gouge out the earth. Mother Earth, Chief! We need to live in a way that respects Mother Earth!"

"Mmm." The Indian deliberately looked away from Wolf and said very carefully, "Respect."

Wolf felt uncomfortable. Had he said something he shouldn't have? He thought about it. "Ah. Okay. So maybe you're thinking that what I was doing to those machines wasn't respectful. But, see, I respect the people who run the machines. They don't know they have any choice. It's the corporations. It's the system. It's the system that I'm at war with."

"Young men always like to make war. It's the first thing they think of."

"I've got to do *something*."

"When word came to me that the young men were planning a raid, I would go to the Bostons and warn them."

"Warn them? Against your own people?"

"Mmm. Young men make trouble." He looked at his feet. "This floor is cold."

Wolf had a thought. He didn't like it. "Did you… Chief, you aren't the one who…"

"Called the Boston soldiers. Mmm."

"The Boston soldiers? You mean the police? You called them? *You*?"

"I got inside the wire. There are things you can do when you're dead. Like this."

And he was gone. Vanished. The edge of the bed was still wet, though. Puddles still glistened on the floor.

Wolf sat thinking for a while. His cell mate still snored. The man had slept through the whole conversation. When the puddles dried, there would be no evidence that Wolf had really spoken to the ghost. But he had. What should he do now?

Raven would never believe this. But Peach might. Maybe, just maybe, there was something in what the Chief had said that would help Wolf figure out what to say to her when the time came. Maybe.

Wolf had some hard thinking ahead of him.

But the one clear lesson was this: Ghosts were real. They were bound to the earth by their famous names.

Wolf went to the door of the cell. He gripped the rigid bars. "Houdini," he whispered. "In the name of Harry Houdini."

Introduction to "Heart of Shanodin"

"Heart of Shanodin" is traditional high fantasy. I was hired to adapt this story as a stage play and assured that production was definite and right around the corner. Over time, I have learned that far more scripts for screen or stage are paid for than are actually used. Money for production of "Heart of Shanodin" vanished overnight as the corporate sponsor had a change of heart. Happily, I was still paid for the script. Unhappily, I never got to see the special effects that the director assured me he would be able to pull off.

Heart of Shanodin

There was no path. The two riders—the heavily armored one astride a great black charger, the gray-clad one upon a leggy horse that looked half like a deer—wove among the towering trees. They rode parallel, but kept at least a sword's reach between them. The gray rider spoke almost without ceasing, and the armored one not at all.

When the knight for once glanced at his companion, he saw a wisp, a snicker, a joke of a man who hid every thought he had behind a grin. What was Daisilodavi but a self-made mystery? You could not know a man like that, who, for all his talking, never came to utter a serious remark. Yet for all his dither and dance, for all his jabber jabber, for all the distracting whirl that kept the real man invisible, Daisilodavi was efficient at his craft. King Amjad, may his name provoke trembling, found the little man indispensable. That was the thing that nagged the knight most of all, that he should have a rival for his lord's dark heart, and that the rival should be one so airy as this.

Daisilodavi, when he looked at the knight riding beside him, saw a lump, a grunt, an iron statue that hid all its secrets in silence. What was Khairt but a stubborn cipher? A man who would answer no questions about his past was not unknowable. Some things about a man's history might be writ, like ciphers, upon his body. But on Khairt, most such signs were hidden beneath his black chain mail. The ragged scar on his cheek spoke of battle, and what was the surprise in that? There was the grindingly slow way he walked, the grunts he made when he must bend his legs. That might have some interesting cause, but what? Khairt would never say. And if Daisilodavi must have a rival for the patronage of Amjad, may his name cause jaundice, why must it be so unreadable a rival as this? Daisilodavi could tease an opinion or an argument out of the man from time to time, but never anything revealing. Even the knight's accent was strange, such a blending of accents that even the place of the knight's birth remained uncertain.

But soon the knight would reveal something of himself. He would have no choice. Smiling, Daisilodavi rose up in his saddle and waved his hand at the deep forest. "Like stars at the end of time," he said.

Khairt, riding beside him, turned his helmeted head neither to the left nor to the right. He knew what the smaller man was talking about, but he made no reply. Like stars littering the forest floor, spots of sunlight flashed here or there among the black and musty leaves. Such glints of sun had been rare enough when the two horsemen first entered the Shanodin Forest. Now Khairt and Daisilodavi had ridden two days among the enormous trunks, and the trees grew ever taller, the high canopy ever thicker, and sunlight ever weaker with every step that brought them toward the Heart of Shanodin. Scattered spots of sunlight grew still more sparse—stars winking out at the end of time.

"Ah, but such a phrase has too much poetry in it for you, does it not?" said Daisilodavi. "You are all glower and doom and words of one syllable and sentences of one word." He lowered his eyebrows in mock seriousness and scowled. "Aye," he said as deeply as he could. After a long pause, he added,

"No." Then he laughed. "And when you have something more than that to say, what is it but some opinion that things are bad and getting worse? You make too much of the name of knight, I think, for you are ever thinking night thoughts. It is daylight! Birds sing! Khairt, don't you ever raise your black eyebrows? Don't you ever open your eyes?"

Still, Khairt said nothing.

"Fah, what a traveling companion you are," said Daisilodavi. "Knight, you're as chatty as a brass man."

It was an apt comparison in more than one sense, for Khairt was armored head to toe. He was so big that even unarmored he'd have needed a heavy mount. With sword and shield and chain mail, he must weigh three times what his companion did. His black charger was two hands taller than Daisilodavi's mount, and stocky as a draft horse. His raised visor showed but a little of his face, which was dark and blunt, the face of a man accustomed to absorbing, unblinkingly, the shocks of battle. His eyebrows were indeed black.

As everything about Khairt suggested heaviness, so did the other man embody the airiness of an elf. The cape covering his slender shoulders was silvery gray, and it billowed in the slightest breeze. Daisilodavi's hair was yellow near to white. His face, smooth and courtly, was young seeming, though there were fine lines etched about his eyes and mouth, and not all of these came of grinning. There was no sign of any weapon on him, no small dagger at his belt, no odd fold in his tunic where a poisoned needle might be tucked. To most he would seem as harmless as he was talkative.

"Perhaps you are indeed a conjured thing," Daisilodavi continued. "That would explain much, for I have never seen you naked of your iron sheath. Perhaps you are empty chain mail with an enchanted head atop." And he reached as if to rap the knight's metal boot and hear if it rang hollow.

Khairt's gauntleted hand closed around Daisilodavi's wrist like a vice, and only when Daisilodavi winced did Khairt release him. The knight said only, "We are watched."

"Of course we are watched," said Daisilodavi, rubbing his wrist. "Eyes have been upon us since the moment we entered the Shanodin, though they are not eyes that have a care for our mission here."

He kicked his horse into a trot, dodging branches as his mount sped him through the trees. "Oh, you watchers!" he cried. "Have you ever seen the likes of me? Has a more graceful rider ever passed among these trees?" And then, with the elegance of a dancing centaur, horse and rider wheeled about and faced Khairt. "Ha!" he cried. "They watch that I might melt their wooden hearts!"

"Take care how you speak," said Khairt.

"Do you fear the ladies of the wood?" Daisilodavi grinned. "Or do you pine for them?" He laughed at his own joke.

Khairt turned his head. "You capering fool," he said, and his voice was hard and cold as the iron chains that keep Yyelor, the ice giant, bound to the frozen north. Even so, Khairt's voice was not so hard and cold as King Amjad's. Nothing, Daisilodavi thought, was so hard and cold as their lord's voice when he was displeased.

Khairt's gauntlet closed tight upon the pommel of his saddle. "Why does this take two of us? Why did Amjad, may his name be feared, not send me alone to slay this Glinham?"

"Shadowy are the ways of Amjad, may his name cause nosebleeds," said Daisilodavi. "Though perhaps the answer is obvious. I have been to the Heart of Shanodin before. You have not."

"I can find my way without you bounding at my side like some not-weaned pup. And I don't need your help."

"Indeed. And I hardly need you along to dispatch this Glinham. Do you think I desire your company? Do you imagine that I pleaded with Amjad to send us out together? You lumber like a plow horse and drag your shadow behind."

"All men drag their shadows," said the knight.

"I mean your sulky silence, your dour words, your second skin of black steel. In short, you are as obvious as an ugly assassin. You are the very thing a man fears. The quarry sees you gallumphing from a distance and readies himself for attack. Whereas I come to him with smiles, find him where he is resting, reassure him, encourage him…"

A blade flashed in the Daisilodavi's hand, sliced the air before him, then vanished before Khairt could guess where it had come from.

"To ride with you," Daisilodavi went on, "is to send out runners before me crying, 'Beware! Trust not this gentle stranger! He comes in the company of death!'"

"Then depart. Go your own way. I will find the one we seek, and when I have finished him, I will find you by the sound of your prattling."

But neither one could leave the other. Amjad's commission had been explicit. They were together to follow this Glinham to the Heart of Shanodin—the man had left broad clues of where he meant to hide—and together kill him. But why together? Was there any reason for Amjad to doubt that either of them, alone, could undo this man, this mere merchant? No reason that Khairt could see, and so he was uneasy with a thing he could make no sense of.

The brambles began as a wild rose here, a stem of blackberry there, widely scattered, but as the riders pressed on, the thorny stems grew thicker and more frequent, until all the ground beneath the trees was woven thick with briers. Daisilodavi's horse shied half a step for every step he coaxed it forward.

Khairt dismounted and unsheathed his broadsword.

"We near our destination," Daisilodavi said. "These brambles guard the Heart."

Khairt stepped slowly forward, then raised the heavy sword and swung. Thorn and leaf flew. He took a step and swung the other way, and soon there was a rhythm to his cutting, a march of stroke and step that tumbled prickly stems like waves before a prow. His knees hurt him, but then they always hurt when he was afoot, and the pain gave him a focus, helped him to concentrate.

Though the stems grew thicker, higher, and tighter woven as Khairt went, there was pleasure in this work, as there was in battle. If he did not turn around, he could imagine that no one stood behind him but his horse. Every so often, Daisilodavi destroyed the illusion with some loud and foolish joke. "And to think I called you witless! Yet here you deal so cuttingly with the barbs set against you!" But Khairt ignored him, considered him gone, and soon again felt peacefully alone in his labor.

Alone but for the eyes of the forest. Even when he imagined that the assassin was not at his back, Khairt could not stop feeling the gaze of the woods upon him.

In the Shanodin, of all the world, a man never walks unseen. That was the saying.

Khairt's shoulders were sore and his breathing labored by the time he broke through the thickest part of the brambles. Now, though, the hewing and hacking grew easier with every step, and soon he was enough into the clear that even Daisilodavi's thin-skinned colt could step between the sparse stems.

Without a word, Khairt leaned a moment on his sword, taking the weight from his aching joints, then returned the broadsword to its scabbard.

"That was well done," said Daisilodavi, "but is not done long."

Khairt did not take his meaning until he turned and saw how the brambles grew and twined to reknit the barrier behind them.

"We've no easier way out than the way we came in, I fear," said the assassin.

"Glinham is trapped. If he is here."

"Oh, he's here," said Daisilodavi. "Rely upon it. He thought this place would save him."

"With so mild a wall of thorns? The man's a fool." Khairt put his hands on armored hips and gazed at the brambles. The stems bore blossoms—white and red and pink. How was it that he had not noticed them 'til now? In the trees above him, a thrush sang sweet a song that minded him of evening, and he found himself thinking of stars crowding in a purple sky…

"Fool indeed," said Daisilodavi, looking hard at Khairt.

The knight, not quite knowing why, dropped his visor before his eyes. Shaking himself, as if from sleep, he took to his horse again. He did not raise the visor until he had ridden a little ways before Daisilodavi, and raised it then only because the forest floor was shot through with flowers. He wanted to see all of them at once.

Above his head, the thrush still sang. Rare sunlight sparkled among the leaves. How had Daisilodavi put it? Like the last stars at the end of time? More like diamonds. More like fires burning on a night sea.

Khairt had slept, and now at last was waking. For how else to explain that now he saw and now he heard? The world was alive with bird song and blossom. How had he forgotten?

Daisilodavi began to sing, and it was not an unpleasant sound, nor even an irritating one, as Khairt usually found it. The assassin sang of green meadows and bright sun, of a maid with spring flowers in her hair. Of a sudden, the singing stopped.

"So thaws the black ice around Khairt's heart," said Daisilodavi, coaxing his horse to draw alongside the knight. "There's a bit of sunlight ashine within his iron breast."

Khairt lowered his brow. It took some effort. He did not feel stony and distant, but he mastered himself enough that his words tolled like a funeral bell when he said, "More nonsense."

"None at all!" said his companion. "You betray your heart, or shall I say your heart betrays you? As I was singing just now, you were nodding your head in time."

"I was not," Khairt said.

"You were. And in a moment you'd have sprung from your horse to dance!"

"If I spring from my horse, it will be to run you through," Khairt said through his teeth.

Daisilodavi laughed and reined his horse, letting Khairt again take the lead. Again he began to sing.

This time, Khairt gritted his teeth and concentrated on thoughts of battle in order to block out the song. He tried to remember all the machines of war he knew and to consider the weaknesses of each. He thought of tactics for single combat, posing himself questions: if armed with a mace, how to proceed against a swordsman? If unhorsed and disarmed, how then to deal with a pikeman? Caught without armor or weapons, how to close with a dagger-wielding foe? With these thoughts, he ignored singer and song, ignored flower and leaf and dappling sun. He concentrated so well on imagined enemies that a true one was upon him before he knew it.

"Blackguards!" cried the blur that sprang from the bushes.

As Khairt turned in surprise, groping for the pommel of his sword, something struck him high. Had the blow come half a second later, he'd have found his balance, readied himself, but instead he slipped from his saddle and tumbled toward the leafy ground.

"To hell!" shouted the voice. Khairt rolled onto his back as his assailant vaulted over his horse.

"What have we here?" Daisilodavi half sang.

What indeed? thought Khairt. The one who had just unhorsed him was little more than a girl, and armed with only a wooden staff. She wore the coarse rags of a scullery maid. A black smudge, as of stove black, marked her cheek.

But the young woman stood in a warrior's stance. She gripped the staff by one end. She swung. The staff arced toward Khairt's unprotected face.

Khairt kicked and rolled in a half-forgotten move. His chain mail slowed him, his left knee throbbed, but the maneuver still worked. The staff struck the earth with a thud, and Khairt was backing onto his feet by the time the girl was ready for another swipe at him.

"Will you not yield?" she demanded.

"Yield?" said Khairt. "To a girl with a staff? Yield?"

"Or die," the young woman said.

"I rather think she means it," said Daisilodavi, bemused. Still mounted, he had sidled behind the lass, but kept his distance.

To Khairt's eye, there was much awkwardness to the way the girl held herself. As spirited a fighter as she might be, she was unschooled. By shifting her weight, or by standing still too long, she revealed openings, opportunities for Khairt to sweep her from her feet.

Yet Khairt did not do so. Instead, he watched her face. Her hair, though plain and brown, swept back on either side like folded wings. Her eyes were bright and clear. There was determination in her face, yet little hardness.

She was beautiful, and though he no doubt had looked upon beautiful women often enough, the last time he had looked and *seen* like this had been...

Oneah.

He clenched his fists. "*You* will yield," Khairt said. "And you will tell us why you waylay strangers."

"You're no strangers to me," she said. "All about you hangs the stink of Amjad."

"May his name cause head lice," said Daisilodavi.

The girl took a step to the side, trying to keep the gray-clad rider from getting behind her, while still keeping the knight before. "I fight to protect my Lord Glinham."

"Then do I grieve for you," said Khairt, "for Glinham must die."

Resolve flashed in her eyes a moment before she moved, and Khairt knew how she would launch herself, and how swing her staff. He dove beneath her attack and struck her knee with his forearm. She swayed. He struck again and swept her from her feet.

She did not fall well. He heard a snap that might have been her wrist as she tried to catch herself. She winced as she rolled aside.

Between the weight of his armor and the creaking of his knees, Khairt could not grasp and pin her. She struggled to her feet, cradling her wrist.

Though Khairt had not even seen the man dismount, Daisilodavi was waiting for her. The needle jabbed the back of her neck before she knew he was near. Before she could turn, he was six steps beyond her, and before she staggered and fell, he had mounted his horse again.

A rictus of agony twisted the pretty face and left it twisted as she died. Khairt looked away.

"That was not needful."

"It was," said the assassin. "She'd never have yielded. Were you to defeat her for the moment, she'd have been hunting us again as soon as she was able. Mayhap she would brain you with a lucky blow, if we let her keep trying."

"She fought like a hero."

"She did," said the assassin, kicking his horse to a walk. "She had the heart of a hero." Over his shoulder he said, "Are you developing a conscience?"

Khairt made himself look at her face again. When was the last time he'd felt the slightest regret in seeing an opponent die? But what he felt was not any pang of conscience. He was only sorry that her face was no longer pretty.

Khairt heaved himself into his saddle again and, at a trot, caught up with Daisilodavi. "If the scullery maid has a hero's heart," he said, "then how much more dangerous must be Glinham's men at arms!"

"In the Heart of Shanodin," said Daisilodavi, "expect surprise."

"I always expect surprise."

"Save for the ambuscade of a scullery maid." Daisilodavi winked. "What were you dreaming of, to let her take you unaware?"

"I do not dream," the knight said through his teeth. He called a harsh "Geha!" to his horse and trotted ahead of his companion.

But the question remained. How *had* he been so easily surprised? How was it that he had fallen into a state of bliss, of satisfaction? If ever a man thinks himself satisfied and happy, then does he open himself to wounds. Khairt knew that well, as he knew also that the man who endures is the man who strikes first, who kills without mercy, who sees any garden as a likely battle ground. What is a hedge but a hiding place? What is a fountain but a place where one's enemies might be drowned?

And yet... Even as these hard thoughts came to him, so came to him the gentle rustling of leaves high above, the surprise of bright blossoms in the undergrowth. He thought again of the girl's face, the brightness of her eyes while she lived.

He took a deep breath and drank in the scents of the forest. The black leaves of the forest floor and the black earth beneath smelled as rich as bread baked fresh. Again, he heard thrush song, and the calls of other birds high above. He felt the eyes of the forest at his back, above, all around.

So it was that, for a second time, he was lost in reverie when Daisilodavi rode up next to him and hailed the man who walked before them. "A fellow traveler," said the assassin. "Did you not see him?" Then, loudly, Daisilodavi called out, "Ho, soldier!" for the man had a short sword strapped to his belt and went along tapping the ground with the end of an unstrung bow. "Ho, archer!"

The man did not turn. His clothes were filthy, as if he'd been sleeping on the bare ground.

"Blue and gold braid on his tunic," said Daisilodavi. "This is Glinham's man. Do you see?"

"I have eyes."

"By the look of him, though," the assassin continued, "he may be no one's man at all."

Khairt's hand rested on his sword. "Surfaces deceive."

"Not always," said Daisilodavi with a thin smile. "Not in all places." Then he called again, "Ho, archer! Thou wanderer, ho!"

The man did not stop or look up until the two riders passed him, one on either side. Daisilodavi spun his mount to face him. Khairt rode a bit further, scanning the bushes for signs of another ambuscade. He saw no threat. However, he did notice the butterflies flitting above the foliage. Their wings were silver on blue—Clouds in Heaven, he'd have called them, were it his task to name them. He leaned forward to see them better.

Stop this! he thought. He was not here for butterflies. He was here to kill a man. With a tug on the reins, he halted and turned his horse.

Daisilodavi was asking the man-at-arms, "And did you not hear us?"

"Aye, whether or not I heard you, that was what I considered," the man said. His hair was tangled and bits of leaves clung to it. "I was thinking, 'Is that voices I hear, and do they hail me?' If I turned to see you, could I then be certain that you existed? What certainty is there in the senses?"

"What's he prattling about?" said Khairt.

"Let him speak," said Daisilodavi.

"I thank you," said the man, "whether you exist or not. As I say, what certainty is there in the senses? Do the mad not see what is not there? Do dreamers not hear and see what they believe to be real? Who is to say that I will not, a moment hence, wake with a start to think what a strange conversation I was having just moments ago in my sleep?"

Daisilodavi smiled. "I take your meaning. And even were you to wake, how could you know that you were not having a dream of waking? Perhaps you are a great sea slug asleep on the ocean floor, dreaming that you are a man, when in truth no such creature as man has ever been."

"Just so."

"Gods and gashes," said Khairt. "I have never heard such nonsense traded." He drew his broadsword from the saddle scabbard, then balanced it on his shoulder. "Answer while you have your head to speak with. Where is your lord?"

"I have no lord," the man said. "I am finished with that life." He lifted his unstrung bow. "Have you considered," he asked, "the impossibility of an arrow's flight?"

"Answer me!" said Khairt, lifting the sword. "Where is Glinham?"

"I can hardly be sure that such a being as Lord Glinham ever existed," the man said, spreading his hands helplessly. "As for where he is now, I do not know, and can not be sure I would know how I knew if indeed I thought that I did know."

Khairt grew red in the face.

"No need to split his head," said Daisilodavi, smiling. "Put away your sword, knight. He answers you as best he can."

"Nonsense!"

"Hardly nonsense," said the man. "Fundamental questions!" For the first time, an almost soldierly flash came to his eyes, but he made no move toward the sword at his belt. It was as though he had forgotten he had it.

"Sword down," Daisilodavi said to Khairt. "We'll find neither help nor hindrance here."

The knight rested the heavy blade on his shoulder again.

"You said something of arrows," said Daisilodavi.

"Arrows," the man said. "Yes. That was the end to my soldiering. Consider, before an arrow can fly to its mark, it must fly halfway, must it not?"

"Indeed," said the assassin.

"And from that point, it must fly again halfway further, true?"

"True."

"And from there, halfway again—an eighth—and from there, halfway to the mark once more—a sixteenth. Wherever it flies, from half to quarter to eighth to sixteenth, the remaining space may be divided again by half. And then by half again. And may it not be infinitely divided? Is the space ever so small that it may not be halved again? So the points through which the arrow must pass are infinite in number. And, being infinite, they may not be summed. The arrow will never reach its mark."

Daisilodavi said, "The fletcher's paradox, that is called."

"Is it? I thought I had originated it."

"Nay, it has wrinkled many brows before yours."

"You see now wherefore I leave my bow unstrung."

"I do."

"Do you?" said Khairt. "Do you think an arrow will not pierce a heart because the archer has bethought this muddle?"

"You, sir," said the man, "are a fool."

"*I*, a fool?" said the knight. "I'll show you who's the fool!"

"Come," said Daisilodavi, turning his horse. "We've a task." Over his shoulder, he called to the former man-at-arms, "Here's a thought for you. Consider that an all-powerful demon appears in your dreams and offers you three wishes. Your first wish is that your first wish not be granted. Has the all-powerful demon the power to grant that wish?"

With a snort, Khairt returned his sword to its scabbard. He did not immediately give the former man-at-arms his back. The fellow still had a sword, after all. He might not be so addled as he seemed.

"I wish that this wish not be granted," the man said to himself. He began to chew his lip and rub his forehead.

Khairt turned his horse. When he caught up with the assassin, he said, "Will you not circle back and poison this one, too?"

"I have poisoned him with a puzzle," said Daisilodavi. "He'll frown upon it until he starves. Or if he gives it up, he'll find another question that wears him down. When he realizes that he is hungry, he'll want a theory of food before he eats. Would that all men were philosophers. Mine would be an easy profession then."

"The world crawls with fools," Khairt said.

"Not fools," said Daisilodavi. "You see not the half of it."

Khairt gave no answer to that. He was already lost in the patterns and variations made by white bark and black, rough and smooth. The very trunks of the trees themselves were a kaleidoscope of shifting geometry as he rode. Only just now had he noticed. As he noticed, he once more felt that his gaze into the trees was returned.

"Not the half," Daisilodavi said.

Dusk light was deepening to gloom when they had ridden far enough to again encounter brambles.

"The far side," said Daisilodavi. "We have ridden the breadth of the Heart of Shanodin."

Shanodin, Khairt thought. It was a beautiful name. There was music to it. But what he said was, "No sign of Glinham himself."

"Oh, there's some sign of him."

"His retainers, you mean."

"No, I mean *him*. Or did you not notice, two or three leagues behind us, a change in the scent of the air? Was there not some unnatural trace?"

Not notice the smell of the air? Why, Khairt had been drunk with it! There were the rich scents of moss and leaf, the musk of a deer somewhere upwind, the sweet notes of flowers, and from some other region of the forest, a subtle scent like vanilla. That was the scent of red-barked Shanodin pines. Nor was that the only spice-like scent. There was a faint trace of attars, as from an alchemist's press—the scent of rose and clove and wanderseed touched with the bite of flame...

Khairt reined his horse. "Lamp oil!"

"So you did smell it. And not any lamp oil, was it? No, someone burns a scented oil, expensive oil. That's the sort of dainty, the sort of luxury we might expect of a rich merchant, aye?"

"Three leagues back! And you did not stop at once?"

"You were so lost in your dreaming, I dared not wake you."

"Dreaming!" Khairt made a fist, but knew not what to insist or what to deny. He had not been dreaming, exactly, though neither had he been about his business. "Demons and dung!" he said at last. "Now I see why our lord Amjad trusts you not to do his bidding!"

"Tell me," said Daisilodavi, "what maze of thoughts were you wandering when that scent came to both our noses?"

"Blast you and your lawyerly graces! Blast your slippery tongue! We should turn and ride. Glinham lies close at hand."

"And so will he at the morrow. It grows dark. We'll encamp and wait for light."

"We might have slain him already," Khairt said. "We might be riding home even now."

"And you want to leave, do you?" said Daisilodavi. "I was thinking that you were somewhat drawn to this place."

The knight looked at the dark shadows of the trees. They seemed both lovely and foreboding. "This forest is too like a woman, and I've had naught to do with women since I left..."

He caught himself before he named the place. In the service of King Amjad, he had never spoken of his life before, in a court upon the plains. The less others knew of his past, the more free he was of it.

Daisilodavi was leaning forward in his saddle, as if straining for the missing word. When it did not come, he dismounted. "There's no sense in risking our horses in the dark. We'll encamp. Glinham is going nowhere in the meanwhile. He has settled, or why do you think we smelled a lamp burning in the day?"

"A cave."

"Quite so. And we'll find the entrance better by day than by night." Daisilodavi laid a blanket upon the ground and unrolled an oilcloth beside it, then went to see to his horse.

Khairt still did not stir from his saddle.

"Will you sleep ahorse?" Daisilodavi said.

"We are watched. Closely."

"And as we do not profane the trees, the watchers mean no harm. Put the dryads out of your mind, knight. Get down. Sleep. I may make use of your sword arm on the morrow."

"None makes use of me but Amjad and I myself. I do not serve you. You make no use of me."

"A figure of speech. Stars in heaven, knight. Dismount and rest!"

Khairt sat a moment longer, lest his immediate response should seem obedience. Then he clambered down, lest his resistance seem only the churlishness of a lesser man. He fed his horse some oats and hobbled it.

The hard tack that had been their meal this week past had passed Khairt's lips untasted day after day. This night, as the last forest light faded, he noticed the fullness of it, the pleasure of so daily a taste as unleavened, unsalted bread.

"Will you sleep sitting up again?" said Daisilodavi. The oil cloth covered him.

"The sooner to my feet and fighting, this way," Khairt said.

"That's if you wake in time. You slept ahorse today. I do not think you'll stand a vigil any better in the night."

Khairt did not answer.

Daisilodavi closed his eyes, and in the darkness, he smiled. The knight was beginning to show himself. At last, Daisilodavi would see what sort of man it was who stood with him at Amjad's right hand.

For his part, Khairt was troubled without knowing quite why. Yes, the feeling that he was ever watched disquieted him a little. But there was something more. Since he had taken up the sword, since he had come into the service of Amjad, a certain calm had settled over him, though he was always in the midst of murder. Or *because* he was always in the midst of murder. Now that calm had left him. He felt naked. Unarmored. There was something more dangerous about this forest than any line of pikemen he had ever charged.

As his eyes grew accustomed to the darkness, he perceived the ghostly glow of phosphorescence on rotting logs and stumps. On many vigils, he had seen this bluish glow, and never fancied it beautiful. Now, as the emberflies and witchbeetles traced lines of red and green light through the black air, he felt as if he'd never seen a greater wonder. Soon he was lost in the weaving patterns of light, and even as his eyes closed, still he saw the lights dance.

He dreamed flowers. He dreamed black tree trunks, and brown, and gray, and white, soaring toward the canopy above like pillars in a great hall. He dreamed of the black swirls and dots and slashes on white birch bark, saw that these markings were lines of poetry he could almost read. His lips, thick with sleep, tried in vain to form the words.

Khairt dreamed of butterflies. He dreamed of brief openings in the canopy, of spots of blue sky glimpsed between the leaves, rare and precious as sapphires.

His arms and legs were leaden. He dreamed of fingers emerging from the tree he slept against, fingers that gently touched his iron rings of chain mail. He dreamed that he sat paralyzed and trusting as more fingers brushed his metal bootguards, worked the hinges of his visor down and up, and tested the weight of his sword.

If this were no dream, his death might be at hand. If these fingers truly played about him, if this being wished him ill...

He tried to move. He could not.

With effort, he opened his eyes. Two green witchbeetles hovered before him, not an handsbreadth apart. Fingers gently traced his eyebrows, moved down to close his eyes. *Those are no witchbeetles*, he thought, drifting deeper.

When next he opened his eyes, gray light had returned to the Heart of Shanodin. Daisilodavi, a lumpen heap beneath his oil cloth, began to stir.

Khairt struggled to his feet. His knees this morning felt filled with broken glass. He grunted.

"And to you, too, a good morrow," said Daisilodavi.

"We had visitors," Khairt said, scanning the ground for tracks. He saw none, but dryads are light upon their feet.

"We're the visitors," said the assassin. "Is it any wonder that they should want to inspect us?"

Inspect they had. Khairt remembered the feel of hands upon his sword. How had he not awakened? How not risen and fought?

Khairt walked stiffly to his horse, sheathed the broadsword, and said, "Let us go and do our killing, then be gone from here."

"Murder, murder, murder. Is pleasure all you ever think of? Oh, thou libertine!"

"I think of getting from this place alive. Arise!"

"Am I a zombie, that you would raise me?"

"From your first words of the day, you prattle."

"From your first words, you are sour. I rise, my knight. Soon we are off to kill. Will you feel better once you have bathed your sword?"

Khairt gave no answer, but bent to unhobble his horse.

As he rode, Khairt concentrated on the purpose of their mission. Yes, the ivy creeping up the trunks was lush, and yes, trills and chatterings of the birds were rich and pleasing. But he must not think of that. He must only think of spilling blood, of the purifying sweat of battle.

Let Glinham be well-armed. Let such men-at-arms who still served him be of great fighting spirit. To fight, to kill, that alone would bring Khairt relief. Damn these butterflies with their varicolored wings! Let these purple flowers fall and rot! May hawks dine upon these songbirds!

But even as he cursed the beauties of the forest, so too did he enumerate them. He could not help but have eyes and ears.

"We are very near the place," said Daisilodavi, halting. "Back this way, I think." He crossed a brook.

The sound of water rushing by the horse's feet was bright as bells. Khairt grimaced. Eyes half closed so that he might concentrate on purifying thoughts of blood, he followed.

The entrance to the cave, once they neared it, was obvious. To say that it lay in a clearing would be to suggest an open sky and bright light shining. There are no clearings in the heart of Shanodin. But for some little space, the trees grew not so crowded, and in the center of that spot was a pile of rock overgrown with vines and creepers.

Both men dismounted. Daisilodavi rummaged in his saddlebags for a lamp, flint, and oil rags.

The opening between the rocks was narrow.

"You're too big a rat for this wee hole," said the assassin as he ignited the rags to light the lamp. "Here is where we must part."

"I can get through," said Khairt.

"Mayhap, if you stripped off that chain mail and greased yourself in bear fat. That will take some time. First you must hunt a bear."

"Armor and all," said the knight, "I can get through."

"And then what? Fight with a broadsword where there may not be a shoulder's breadth to swing it? Nay. Stay here. Keep a watch. Perhaps I'll flush the quarry out, and then he will be yours."

"If he is well guarded, what chance have you?"

"I daresay he is not guarded well. No matter how many men-at-arms he brought with him here, I'll wager that the one true soldier was that girl we slew. The rest will have deserted him."

"Why?"

"You are ever slow to understand, Khairt. Stand you here a while and think on it." With that, he disappeared into the hole.

Khairt did not stand long, though. His knees ached. He sat on a stone and watched the entrance of the cave, listened for any sound from the assassin.

From the black hole, he heard nothing. It was as though the earth had swallowed Daisilodavi up. But all around him, Khairt again heard the music of bird song. He inhaled the forest scents, and of a sudden the helmet on his head felt like a cramped, confining room. He pried it off. Fresh air against his skin felt as good as it smelled.

Khairt looked again at the cave entrance. The hole might be no deeper than an oubliette. Then again, it might stretch for miles. Daisilodavi could be days in flushing the quarry, if, indeed, he did not simply kill Glinham where he found him.

In an hour, it was clear that the hole was no oubliette.

Khairt knew that he should wait here, helmet on, sword at the ready, like a sentinel. But his hair felt oily, and his skin was sticky with sweat.

He bethought himself, then, of the brook.

The narrow fracture that admitted Daisilodavi narrowed further, until he could just wriggle forward inches at a time.

Then the crack widened, grew round, and opened gradually into a wide and level passage. The walls, though smoothed by the tumble of ancient waters, were dry, and the floor was dusty. This cave had long been dead. Here, no waters dripped from the ceiling to grow crystals or stalactites.

The passage gave way to a large room. The sharp smell of guano told of bats crowding the far reaches of the ceiling, beyond the yellow glow of Daisilodavi's lantern. His glow caught the glimmer of something on the floor, and he discovered a little mound of jewelry—a man's heavy golden bracelet, rings set with fine stones. He slipped the bracelet onto his wrist and put the coins in the pocket of his cape.

Then he listened.

Silence.

The tunnel continued on the far side of the room. This passage led to yet another, smaller room, but one that made Daisilodavi sit down and consider, for in this room, with his lamp raised high, the assassin could see no fewer than five openings that promised further passages.

It would do him no good to sniff the air that issued from each. The spiced oil had been burning for some time inside the cave, and the smell had by now bled into every room and tunnel. Besides, the fumes of his own lamp were much the stronger smell. So which way to go?

Then he heard the chanting.

At first, Khairt had only splashed water on his face, rubbed the drops from his eyes, and looked warily at where his chain mail lay spread across a fallen trunk. Nearer at hand was his sword.

When no one crept from behind a tree to fling a stone or rush him with a staff, he dared to lower his brow to the running stream. He rose. Cool water ran from his hair, down his cheeks and onto the back of his neck. His clothes, worn these many days beneath the armor, were filthy.

Not far upstream, an emerald finch landed on the shallow bank, cocked its head to consider Khairt, and them began to bathe in a patch of sunlight. Droplets rolled from its back and shivered from its wings like diamonds.

Khairt took a deep breath and began to strip. As he laid his black clothes down, as he gave himself over to the open air, it was as though he were laying aside a dream. Naked, he walked downstream until the found a pool deep enough to lie in. First he washed the sweat-crusted clothes. Then he knelt in the current, filled his palm with water, and dribbled it over the flower tattoos on his arms, over the varicolored bird tattoos on his chest.

He sank into the water. The hair on his legs obscured the brown tattoos, but it was still obvious enough that those lines were meant to represent tree bark. "Let my legs be like the oak," he had told the tattoo master. And there had been prophecy in his choice. In every match, his legs had been rooted to the ground. He'd been impossible to move, no matter how the other wrestlers might kick at his knees. Immobile he had stood, waiting for his opening, waiting for the shift that would let him drop and pin his opponent or spin him out of the ring.

Like the oak, he was unbending. And like the oak, when at last he must yield, since he could not bend he must break. In one match, two body blows to his knees ended his career.

Khairt rolled in the water, letting the stream rush over and around and through. He stretched, luxuriated, and at last rose, dripping.

If before the flowers in the underbrush were colorful, now they were brilliant. If before the thrush's song had seemed beautiful, now it was enthralling. Butterflies danced in vibrant clouds.

"Eyah!" Khairt cried three times, an Oneahn exultation. He shook his head, raining water and delight. He stamped his bare foot down on the leaves, ignoring the protest of his knee. "Koy!" he called out. "First approach!" And he stepped across the ground in the first gait of his school, the first balanced walk that he had learned.

"Izza!" he cried. "First turn!" He turned three quarter turns, always rooted to the ground.

The more complicated moves then came to him as easily as breath, though he had not practiced them for long years. These steps, The Dance That Breaks Bones, were not truly a wrestler's moves. Within the court, they were forbidden, for these moves were not sport, but the warrior's art.

Khairt took a running step, leaped into a winged side kick, and landed on one leg.

His knee quivered. He bit back the pain, but remained standing. He managed to pivot, and then he was into the next move, the sweeping gestures that made him think of waves. Ah, he was dancing. He began the Walk of Spinning Pins, turning and turning as he crossed the forest floor. Now he was alive as long he had not been. Ittono Khairt ni Hata Kan, Grand Champion of the Court, dances once more, and in his dancing lives the Court of a Thousand Thousands…

Green eyes.

One turn more, and one turn more, and…

Green eyes.

He stopped turning. Someone was watching him.

Khairt turned around in the other direction, a little dizzily, and with his knees now throbbing with pain.

There. Across the brook, in the shadowed ivy there, between those trees. Two lights shone like the green glow of witchbeetles, not a handsbreadth apart.

She blinked, stepped forward, and only when she moved thus did he really see her. It was as though she'd been invisible, though now he knew he'd seen her all along, yet not known her feet from roots nor her arms from branches. He'd not known how to see her.

The more she moved, the more plainly he saw her. Her arms did not end in branches at all, but in hands like his. Her feet were feet, not roots. How had he seen her skin as tree bark, when it was only tattooed in that pattern, like his legs?

Her eyes, in truth, did not glow like witchbeetles. They were green, though, and filled with ordinary light. She smiled, and Khairt did not know if ever he had seen a woman so beautiful. Not even the courtesans of Oneah had been her like.

Beautiful, yet dangerous, also, should he give offense. He watched her warily.

She turned a circle, stopped, then looked at him, a question in her eyes.

Khairt shrugged. She repeated the motion.

"Ah!" he said. "The Walk of Spinning Pins!" He smiled. "No, no. Not at all like that. Your knee must rise to the level of your hip. And point your toes, so." And he turned for her, then watched as she repeated the move. "Yes," he said. "That's better. Now, mind your hands." He turned for her again, and then she turned as he had shown her, and soon the two of them were dancing The Walk of Spinning Pins on either side of the brook. They danced as far as the place where Khairt's black clothes lay drying on a bush.

"Gods and gashes!" he cried, remembering his nakedness and snatching up the clothes. At that, the dryad vanished.

Khairt gazed at the spot where she had been. Then he laughed and shook his head. "My apologies, lady of the wood," he said. "I am unaccustomed to dancing without a breechcloth." He tore his wet tunic to fashion one, but she did not soon reappear.

Daisilodavi stopped now and then to listen to the sound of a man's voice as it rose and fell in the rhythms of a prayer chant. The sound had been growing steadily louder, and now the assassin could sometimes hear something about the *quality* of the sound. The voice was echoed, and not with the sharp echo of a tunnel. This was the resonant, droning echo of a great room.

And he was almost there.

He stopped for a moment to lower the wick of his lamp so that only the tiniest blue flame flickered on the tip, then crept forward a little distance without the light.

At the end of this tunnel, he could just make out an orange glimmer. He went back, raised the wick, and checked to see that all his needles and blades were where they should be. When he continued, he went whistling the tune of a merry drinking song at a much faster tempo than the chant.

The chanting stopped.

Daisilodavi went on whistling. Just before he entered the great cavern, he broke into song:

"If the maid be merry,
and if the maid be strong,
and if she'll fetch and carry
then I'll marry her anon,
hey, marry her anon."

Then, as he stepped into the open, he laughed giddily. "Marry her! Sooner drown myself!" Then he laughed again.

The great room was even larger that the first he had passed through. At the far end of it, high atop a mound of boulders, there burned a lamp, but there was no one to be seen nearby.

"Ho, did my ears deceive me, or did I hear prayers issuing from here? Hey and hullo, is there a holy man about?"

No answer came.

Daisilodavi squinted. He could make out a ledge, a sort of shelf that ran around the great room at the level of the lamp.

"What do you want?" asked a voice. Because of the echo, Daisilodavi could not tell where it issued from.

"I want wine," Daisilodavi said. "I have been *days* without wine. Have you any?"

"'Wine is the bane of reason.' So spake the Prophet Eziir."

"Ah, yes. Well, of course it would be unreasonable to expect you to have any, then. Beer, then? Ale?"

"'Drink not of strong spirits, nor of wine, nor of any fermented drink, lest in body and in spirit ye shall die.'" The voice echoed. "So spake the Prophet Haprina in her sermon to the kings. So accounted are the Words of the Prophets."

"Ah, I see how matters stand, then," Daisilodavi said. "I've little hope of wine. Well, then, Lord Glinham, you'll not object if I ask only to sit and rest, will you?"

"You speak a name that has fallen away."

"Of course, of course. You've a new name now, I suppose. A hermit's name."

There was no answer from the voice. Daisilodavi scanned the ledge above, but he could see no sign of exactly where Glinham might be.

"Why have you come?" asked the voice.

"Would you believe," said Daisilodavi, "to do murder?" And he giggled into his sleeve. "Oh, I found this bracelet and other baubles." He let lamp light play over the gold. "But I ought not tell you, for then you'll want them back, will you not?"

"Those are like the skin of the snake, shed with a former life. I do not want them."

"Turned ascetic, have you?" Daisilodavi set his lamp down on the floor of the cave. "From fat merchant to hermit?"

"'The riches of the earth weigh to a holy man as stones weigh in the pockets of him who drowns.' So spake the Prophet Pringle in the Age of the Silver Sun."

For a long moment, Glinham was silent. Then he asked, "Have you still come with murder on your mind?"

"The Heart of Shanodin changes a man," Daisilodavi observed.

"It makes him true," Glinham agreed.

"So spake the prophets."

"In truth, no. The prophets were silent upon matters of the Shanodin Forest. But the Seer Odamulus wrote of this place. 'In Shanodin's Heart,' wrote he, 'a man lives his heart of hearts and follows the path that he wills not or dares not. In Shanodin's Heart, all hearts are revealed.'"

"And thus, when you offended Amjad, may his name be cause for drinking, you came here. Whosoever Amjad would send must become his true heart in the Heart of Shanodin. A wise choice. A merry choice. A strategy worthy of toasting!" Daisilodavi looked about the floor of the cavern. "Did you not, perhaps, discard some wineskins as you discarded your jewels? Is there nowhere hereabout a drop to drink?"

"No wine," said the priestly voice of Glinham. "And as for the wisdom of my choice, aye, there is wisdom to it, but folly as well. Here I have discovered my true heart as a man who would walk the path of the prophets. But what do the prophets demand? 'From him who has seen the light, let shine forth the light, that it may fill not his eyes alone.' Thus spake the Prophet Eziir."

"The words of the prophets are too subtle for me."

"It means that I must shine forth. I must go out into the world and show the light of the prophets to others. But if I leave Shanodin, my former nature will be reborn. Out in the world where I must bear witness to the light of the prophets, my eyes will dim again. My concerns will return to gold and sweetmeats and silken clothes."

"I see," said Daisilodavi. "As the pendulum swings from side to side, so do you swing between prophets and profits."

Glinham did not laugh. "Outside of Shanodin," he said, "I shall be no more priestly than you shall remain a wine-thirsty harmless fool."

With that, Glinham stepped out of the shadows. He had been near his burning lamp all along. He wore a silken tunic, the edges ragged where he had torn away the fine embroidery. There was deep gloom in his voice when he said, "If I leave, I can not remain true to the prophets. Yet if I would remain true to the prophets, I must not stay."

"'Tis sad, this puzzle," said Daisilodavi. He sighed loudly. "None but the Shanodin-enchanted for you to preach to. No one to hear your holy words." He sighed again. "Sorrow was always best washed down with wine. Not a drop, are you sure?"

"What did you say?"

Daisilodavi brightened. "Ah, so you *do* have wine!"

"No, no. Before that. About the Shanodin-enchanted. Why, there's *you*, of course! I have *you* to preach to!"

Daisilodavi picked up his lamp and began to back away. "Not if there's no wine-drinking in your sanctuary. No, no words of the prophets for me, thank you!"

As Daisilodavi turned to flee, Glinham scrambled awkwardly down the tumbled boulders. "Wait! Wait!" he cried. "Prayer is better than wine! You'll see!"

When his knees would bear no more capering, Khairt sat beneath a tree, facing the brook. The forest's sounds, its musty perfumes, its wind-shifted light filled his heart, and ere long he was dancing again, though only from the waist up. As he sat, he let his arms twine in the figures of the Dance That Breaks Bones, and then in other forms he knew. Then he improvised, letting the light and shadow of the forest or the teasing call of a jay suggest a ripple of his great arms, a curling and uncurling of his fingers.

In the brush and shadows across the brook, he saw a branch wave in time with his arm. When he fluttered his fingers, leaves rustled in imitation. He smiled. Still sitting, he swayed from side to side and twisted, and a tree trunk seemed to do the same although, a moment later, it was no tree trunk at all, but her. Her eyes blazed green again, and then were only mortal eyes. She lifted her leg and danced, mirroring what he did with his arms.

"Lady, lovely lady, lovely maid," said Ittono Khairt ni Hata Kan. "Of all the tapestries that hung in Oneah, none there was to match your forest ivy. Of all the musicians that played before the kings of a thousand thousands, none could bring forth the notes of the thrush. Lady, of all the maids I ever bowed to, of all the ladies ever I loved, none was such as thee."

If she understood, she made no sign. She only danced on, even after Khairt's arms grew suddenly heavy and he paused to watch. His breathing grew slow and deep. She danced to the very bank of the brook, and only when his eyelids grew heavy and began to close did he see her smile.

There was something more he wanted to say then. There was some line of poetry he wanted to recite, but his tongue lay heavy in his mouth and would not move. *Do I sleep?* he wondered. *Let me not sleep. Let me not miss, by sleeping, a moment of her presence.*

But if he was sleeping, at least he was dreaming that she was near, for he felt fingertips tracing the birds and flowers of his tattoos. Gently, gently, in his dream, fine fingers traced the lines of bark that decorated his legs.

There was pleasure in her touch, but he bethought himself of danger, too. Should she mean him harm, he was helpless to defend himself. Was a dryad not a creature of the forest? Like a bear, might she not turn from curious to fierce?

He willed his eyes to open. They would not.

And still he willed it. He was a man who had stayed within the ring to finish his final match, though one knee already would not support him. With strength such as that, he willed his eyes to open.

Green lights.

Gently, she made him close his eyes.

Glinham stared at the blood pooling in his palm.

Daisilodavi's dagger glinted in the yellow light. "There's slow poison on the tip," he said. "It seemed a mercy. Though you'll endure some pain, at least you've an hour or so in which to make your peace, to find your consolation in the prophets."

In the assassin's other hand, a needle appeared. "I can give you the quick, if you prefer. Still more pain, but then it's over in an instant."

Tears welled in Glinham's eyes. "H-how?"

"By which you surely mean," said Daisilodavi, "how do I escape the Shanodin's effects? After all, the Heart has made a holy man of you, who before worshiped only gold."

"Not so! I loved the words of the prophets, but only feared to live by them." He clutched his wrist. "How it burns!"

"Howsoever. All of your retainers were changed, and my own companion, who awaits me, he is becoming something else, not the brute slayer of men my Lord Amjad so loves. So how do I escape? How does Daisilodavi remain Daisilodavi? Is it really so hard a riddle?"

Glinham looked again at his wound and bit his lip. His hand began to shake, and he closed his fist.

"True, you've other matters to think upon, and so I will solve it for you. You see, Amjad himself brought me here once, for he would know the hearts of those who closely serve him. And he said it thus: 'As thou art poisonous and merry without, so art thou poisonous and merry within.' Or to put it another way…"

The assassin leaned close to the wincing Glinham. "I act. I lie. I pretend. I change my seeming in a blink of an eye. So what lies beneath? What is the true nature that I guard by my dissembling?" He smiled. "I am an actor. A liar. A pretender. My single nature is that I have no single nature."

"To greet the eye of heaven, that is sweetness," groaned Glinham. "So spake the Prophet Niptea as she burned."

"Did she really?" marveled Daisilodavi.

"The quick poison!" Glinham pleaded. "Give me the quick!"

✦ ✦ ✦

Khairt heard him coming. Or, rather, he heard the silences of the erstwhile singing insects, circles of silence that moved as the assassin moved. Khairt knew when Daisilodavi stood regarding his chain mail, knew when he was looking at the mound of black clothes. Long before Daisilodavi stood over him, Khairt felt his presence.

"Oneahn," Daisilodavi said. "So that's it. A lover of beauty in the Court of Oneah. No wonder I didn't know your accent. That race of men is all but dead."

Khairt opened his eyes.

"We've finished what we came for," said the assassin. "Our lord awaits us with still more bloody deeds."

"I am staying here," Khairt said.

"Knight, you've no choice in the matter. You are sworn to Amjad's service."

"Go. He has deadly enough hands in those two of yours."

"Ah, but we are not the same. Mine are the hands that strike unseen, but he needs yours, too. He may not always strike by stealth."

"I am no longer his."

"You would be," Daisilodavi said. He looked around him. "You would be, were the curse of this place but lifted."

"It is no curse. I am come home. Please, leave me, Daisilodavi." He took a deep breath. "In this forest even *your* name has music to it." He said the name again.

"And you accuse *me* of prattle," said the assassin.

"Once I lived at the center of the world, Daisilodavi, for such was the Court of a Thousand Thousands. I thought that I lived at the heart of beauty. To wrestle was beautiful. To stand in the glimmering court beneath the Roof of Lights was beautiful. And the women of the Court…"

"That is long since past."

"Aye. For me it was passing with the strength of my body. But I thought it would yet stand beautiful forever, before the Goblin War."

Daisilodavi looked away. "You need speak of it no more."

"Why? Is this not why Amjad bade you bring me here, so that he might know my heart? Listen, that you may tell it well. When the Cities and Court of a Thousand Thousands fell, I thought I would never look upon beauty again. Thought I, If all things come to dust, then shall I be the ally of dust. That is why I wandered far until I found a master who would teach me the art of broadsword. Edged weapons were forbidden in Oneah. Sin resides in steel. I no longer cared. I designed to be as black of heart as any goblin." With that last word, his voice shook. With fury, he said, "Let Amjad look upon me, even Amjad, and fear!"

"That's the Khairt I know!"

Khairt laughed. "No longer. I have looked again upon beauty, and I conclude thus, Daisilodavi: That beauty, even more than dust, shall endure."

"Nay," said the assassin. "All things come to dust."

"Not the song of birds. Not sunlight. Leave me. Leave me to the gaze of the forest."

"You do not fear the dryads, then?"

Khairt smiled. "One may know fear, yet not be mastered by it. Only a fool would not fear her."

The assassin nearly said something, then checked himself. "I see," he said. He took a few steps away, then stopped to say over his shoulder, "Dust shall conquer thee, Khairt. Even more than beauty, dust shall endure."

Then he was gone.

Khairt danced and practiced in the last hour of light, and though she did not appear, he knew she watched him.

"Green, more rich than gold, my heart is green," he said. That was the line of Oneahn poetry he had meant before to recite to her. He wished he could remember the rest of the poem, but it was gone. Gone, as all Oneah was now gone.

He must not think of what he had lost. Those were the thoughts of his dark and damaged self. Thoughts of death and ruin did not belong in this place. The Heart of Shanodin was life itself.

When the gloom deepened, he rested against a tree to wait for her. His arms, as before, grew heavy. As before, he could not keep his eyes open.

Near. She was very near.

Feather-light, she touched his skin.

After this dream, his waking dream of her, he dreamed of flower-covered prairies, the sweet plains of his youth.

He woke to a familiar voice.

"High time you were stirring," said Daisilodavi. He was sitting on a log. "It's past first light. We've a long ride today to get out of this forest!"

Khairt rubbed his eyes and stood. "I thought you gone."

"I was gone," Daisilodavi said. "I returned." He threw black rags at Khairt's feet. "Dress. You'll not want to sit ahorse naked. And put your armor on. We may have a fight anon, if we do not ride hard."

"I have no enemies here," Khairt said.

"You do now," Daisilodavi said. "We both do." And as he rose, Khairt saw the shape of the log he'd been using for a bench—the curved calf, the flaring hips, the shoulder.

Khairt groaned, not believing. He rose, knees cracking, and went to turn her, to see the contorted face in the wood.

"Her sisters will not care for details," Daisilodavi said. He grunted as he saddled Khairt's horse. "When they miss her, they'll find this place. There is no judiciary of dryads, no appeal. They'll overnumber and destroy any mortals they soon find near this murder spot."

Khairt gave no warning. Had he moved like the knight Daisilodavi knew, the assassin might have dodged him. But Khairt crossed the ground in the sprinting dance of Ittono Khairt ni Hata Kan, and his knees did not betray him. In half a blink, his hand was at the assassin's throat, and he had the man bent backwards across his other arm. From the corner of his eye, Khairt saw the needle poised in Daisilodavi's hand.

They looked into each others' eyes. With a squeeze of Khairt's hand and a shift of his arms, Daisilodavi's throat would be crushed and his back, broken. With a dying jab of his hand, Daisilodavi could kill the knight wrestler.

"Why?" Khairt said through his grimace. "Do you hate me as your rival? But I would be your rival no longer! Why! You killed her to destroy me!"

Daisilodavi, choking, managed to gasp out, "No. To keep you."

Khairt looked into the man's eyes, then let him drop to the forest floor. Without a word, he picked up the black rags, shook them out, and began to dress.

North of Shanodin, on the Plain of Suns, the grasses waved in the wind.

There was no path. The two riders—the armored one astride a black charger, the gray-clad one upon a leggy horse—wove among the grassy waves.

They rode parallel, not a sword's reach apart. Neither looked to the left nor to the right. They did not speak. Not even as the plains gave way to marshes, then to swamps. Not even as they reached the foul and blighted bogs of their Lord Amjad.

May his name cause silence.

Introduction to "A Common Night"

"A Common Night" is one of my favorite stories, and one of the least known. It has never been reprinted in English. Perhaps because of the heavy use of verse, no translator has attempted it (though there have been some nibbles of interest in France). In short, the story is an orphan, and I'm very happy to see it adopted into this collection.

A Common Night

"So it's another one of her sunset poems," the young woman said, managing to make it sound partly like a question and partly like a bold assertion so that Julian could decide for himself which it was. She gave him a neutral look.

He looked past her, out the second story window to the bare tree outside. Snowflakes were falling.

"Next to 'Leaping like Leopards,' this one seems obvious," said another student, the one with short-cropped black hair. Randal. Or was it Roger? Five weeks into the semester, Julian would ordinarily have had their names down by now.

"I mean, the spots are a clue," Randal or Roger continued. "'She died at play, Gamboled away Her lease of spotted hours…' When I get to those spots, it reminds me of the one we did last week." He flipped pages and read,

> Blazing in Gold and quenching in Purple
> Leaping like Leopards to the Sky
> Then at the feet of the old Horizon
> Laying her spotted Face to die

"That's one thing I like about reading her," Randal said. "Once you've figured out a few of the poems, you sort of have an idea of what she's up to. It's almost fun."

Two or three in the seminar circle laughed at his *almost*.

"I just don't see why she has to work death into every other poem," the young woman continued. "She's so *morbid*."

No one said anything. For an unnaturally long time, the students waited for Julian to stick up for Emily Dickinson.

"Well," he said, but then the next word was very difficult to find. He kept staring at the window, at the falling snow. "Well," he said again.

He had stopped sleeping several nights ago—two or three. He wasn't sure. For weeks, he'd slept fitfully amidst the daily rounds of Home-Hospice-Campus-Hospice-Dinner-Hospice with the kids. Lately he would lie awake all night, listening to the dark, closing his eyes, but never drifting off.

He blinked and looked away from the window. "Death was rather more present in the nineteenth century," he said. "More ordinary, I mean. We tend to hide it away, but death and thoughts of death were more routine."

"But why dwell on it?" the young woman asked.

He looked at the book in his hands. It was full of words, and it was his job now to summon up some more of them, to use Dickinson to explain Dickinson. He could do it. Even after days without sleep, he could do it, but he noticed what a hollow exercise it had become. Whatever he might say next would sound good and satisfying, but it was just a stream of words.

"Let's look at 675 again," he said, and before they had finished turning their pages he recited the first stanza from memory.

Essential Oils— are wrung –
The Attar from the Rose
Be not expressed by Suns— alone –
It is the gift of Screws –

"There's a lot packed into the eight lines of this poem," he said, "and we've already talked about how it seems to be about the poems themselves. But you can think about this as a wider metaphor, too. Attar isn't expressed by suns. That is, you don't get essential oils, you don't get the essence of reality by waiting around for it. You have to squeeze it out. Getting the essential oils out is tough on the rose, but it's the only way."

"And thinking a lot about death is a way of squeezing," said Randal.

"I can enjoy life without thinking about death all the time," another student said. "I agree with Chrissie. These poems are such downers. I don't like being depressed."

Julian thought of Von Trepl's dialogue with Death. Don't blame me for the anguish you're feeling, Death told the Plowman of Bohemia. Your anguish is your own fault. If you had restrained your love for your wife, you'd be free of sorrow over her death. The greater the love, while you hold it, the greater your pain in the end. Unpleasure follows pleasure.

Anna was not dead, but she was already lost to Julian. He had sought out the old German text when the tumor had overtaken the speech centers of her brain. She still recognized Julian, but she couldn't speak. The bridge of words between them had burned, and there were things that still needed saying, would always need saying. Holding her hand as she lay watching him was not enough.

But he didn't mention The Plowman of Bohemia to the seminar. Why bother? It was all just words. Dickinson, too, just words from the dead. Empty, empty. The more he had studied dead words, the more dead they had become. It was the words of the living that mattered, and those had run out. He didn't know if the dead words of literature would ever have anything to do with him again.

"There's a poem I read last night," Randal said, "that I think fits. It's 1100." He found it and began to read.

Julian's attention drifted to the window again. Was that a cat in the tree? But it was gone, the round head vanishing almost as soon as Julian had made out the shape.

> The last Night that She lived
> It was a Common Night
> Except the Dying—this to Us
> Made Nature different
>
> We noticed smallest things –
> Things overlooked before
> By this great light upon our Minds
> Italicized—as 'twere.

The young man's voice droned on as the snow fell outside the window. The words blended and fell in on one another and his voice blended and mixed with the voice of the departmental secretary as she was saying, "Dr. Preston? Excuse me, Dr. Preston?"

Julian looked away from the window. Randal had stopped reading some moments ago, and Julian was aware that he'd gone on staring out the window for some time after the secretary's interruption. The secretary stood in the doorway, as if she had no right to cross the threshold. "Dr. Preston," she said, "there was an emergency call for you." She held a slip of paper.

"Yes," Julian said. It was time. Anna was going. He felt relieved, and then ashamed. "Yes, all right."

Julian's mother-in-law had made the call from the hospice. She would collect Yvonne from school and Nick from day care and meet him.

As he drove out of town toward the hospice, the snow fell thick and fast. It swirled in his headlights and sometimes blew in the same direction that he traveled. In his daze, it seemed that the car was standing still, that the wheels rolled and bumped but somehow didn't carry him forward. He took his foot from the accelerator again and again, tried his brights, though that was worse. He opened his eyes very wide and fought to stay awake and on the road.

There was no other traffic, and it was dark, astonishingly dark for the early afternoon. Why did the hospice have to be a dozen miles out of town? But he knew the answer to that. He understood.

He almost missed the turn-off. The lights of the hospice were just barely visible from the road. The parking lot had not been plowed, and Julian half drove, half sledded to the far corner of the lot, away from the other cars.

When he turned off his lights and killed the engine, the light outside seemed to shift. It was dark, but not too dark to see by. There was a sort of blue-gray glow to the woods that surrounded the parking lot.

Now that he could release it, Julian felt how heavy the burden of staying alert and focused had been. He wanted to melt into his seat and keep on melting. Something gnawed in his stomach, and he realized that he was hungry. Famished. He couldn't remember eating breakfast—he'd been so busy getting the kids ready for school and day care. Had he eaten lunch?

They'd have something for him inside, if he asked. They were so good at this place, terribly good at noticing, terribly good at being concerned for everyone involved.

He closed his eyes. He should go in. They were waiting for him—his son, his daughter, his mother-in-law. He wondered about Anna, wondered if his wife had already…

But he'd know in a bit. He'd go in.

Right now, though, he wanted, for just a moment, to rest here, to let all the effort fall away. He could hear the snow falling, hissing gently, gently, a cottony sound...

A bell jangled.

He opened his eyes. The window was open, and snow was blowing into the car.

The bell jangled again. He squinted into the darkness, and he could see that there was an old-fashioned telephone mounted on the tree next to his car. When the bell jangled a third time, he got out of the car to answer it.

"Yes?" he said. "Hello?"

"Julian?" said the tinny voice in the earpiece.

"Anna?"

"Julian?"

"Anna? Is it really you?"

"Julian?" she said, and there was no doubting that it was her.

"Anna! Anna, sweetheart!"

"Julian?"

"Yes, it's me!" he said. "Oh, God, Anna!" He felt weak with relief. He could hardly stand. "It's so good to hear you!"

"Julian?"

"Can't you hear me? I can hear you fine. Anna?"

"Julian?"

"Anna!" he shouted into the mouthpiece.

Only there wasn't any mouthpiece, just a knot hole in the tree that he had wrapped his arms around.

An orange glow came and went, and a voice from behind Julian said, "Bad connection?"

He turned. He saw nothing but trees.

"Bad connections won't do you any good, you know," said the voice. "In this world, who you know is a big part of who you *are*." Then the orange glow returned, allowing Julian to make out an enormous caterpillar sitting on a tree branch and smoking a long hookah. The glow came from the tobacco burning in the bowl.

"And by the way," the Caterpillar went on, "Who *are* you?"

When Julian didn't answer, the Caterpillar said, "Well, speak up!"

"I'm dreaming," Julian concluded.

"Yes, yes, of course you are," said the Caterpillar. "Or else someone is dreaming you. You can't tell until the very end! But in the meantime, you might be civil."

Julian pinched himself, or dreamed that he pinched himself. The pain felt real enough, and the Caterpillar was still there.

"I'm Julian Preston," he said, giving in. "Professor of English."

"Professor *in* English, you mean," said the Caterpillar.

"*Of* English."

"Don't be rude. I heard you, just a moment ago, profess to be Julian Preston, and you didn't do it in Latin."

"I mean that I teach poetry."

"I'm not surprised," said the Caterpillar. "Poetry has a thing or two to learn. It has more feet than I do and they're terribly difficult to keep track of. 'A was an archer, who shot at a frog; B was a butcher, and had a great dog.' When you say that one, you ought to beat your chest."

"Why?"

"It's written in Pectorals."

"That's not the right term."

"No?"

"No, but at the moment the correct term slips my mind."

"So *you* say. You've only professed *in English* to know poetry. I think you ought to repeat some. Know any Dickinson?"

"Of course," Julian said, and he recited:

Because I could not stop for Toast –
Toast kindly stopped for me –
And brought along a shapely Egg –
And Jam and Juice and Tea.

We chatted long—Toast knows so much
And speaks of all it knows,
Such matters as the Feat of Rhymes
And whether Verse has Toes –

Then round about began to dance
The Toast as it talked on
Of how each day gets started with
The Yeasting of the Sun –

Toast passed the Juice, then passed the Tea –
At last Toast passed the Milk –
The Toast went racing by them all
Until at last I spoke –

Said I—This is all interesting
Or would be if I knew
How it relates to Any Thing
I think or am or do –

But as I haven't dined as yet
And as you're toasted Bread –
Instead of puzzling out your Thoughts
I'll eat you up instead.

"That is not said right," said the Caterpillar.
"It does sound a *little* off," Julian admitted.
"It is wrong from beginning to end," said the Caterpillar decidedly, "and revealing, too. I expect you forgot to eat breakfast today."

"I may have. I feel as though there are a lot of things I'm forgetting. When I was speaking to my wife a little while ago, I was quite surprised to be hearing from her, but I don't remember *why*."

"Ah, *that*," said the Caterpillar. "Well, it will be clear soon enough. Not that clarity helps."

"I don't follow you."

"I didn't ask you to, did I?" said the Caterpillar. It put the hookah into its mouth and began smoking again. Then it yawned, shook itself, got down from the branch and crawled away over the black carpet of fallen leaves. "You've got to go deeper in to get further out," it said. "That's the nature of the tulgey wood."

"The tulgey wood?"

"Where you *are*!"

"Where you are!" said another voice, as if in Julian's ear. He turned, but this time he was quite sure that there was nothing before him but the trees.

"And as long as you are," said another nearby voice, "you've got to be somewhere."

"Until you *aren't*," said a third voice, "and sooner or later you won't be."

"Won't be what?" said Julian.

"Whatever you *are*," said the first voice.

"Or anything else, for that matter," said the third.

Julian wasn't sure, but he thought it might be the trees themselves that were speaking to him. They seemed to sort of sway in time with the words.

"I wish I could see you," Julian said. "It's awfully dark."

"Awfully splendidly," said the first voice.

"Awfully wonderfully," said the second.

"Awfully terribly beautifully dark," said the third. "Too dark to see the stars!"

"No stars! How de*light*ful!" said the first.

Now Julian was positive—the voices were indeed coming from the trees, and they were swaying as they spoke. Not only did they sway from side to side, but the bare branches moved like arms. One branch bent down and pushed Julian backwards. Before he could protest, another was pushing him in the same direction.

"Careful!" he said. "I can't see where I'm going!"

But the trees showed no sign that they heard him. They kept pushing him toward a part of the forest that was, if anything, darker than where he already was. And as the branches shoved him, the tulgey wood sang in voices that varied as he moved past different trees:

Beautiful Dark in heaven so wide
Through thine emptiness we glide
How to escape you? There's nowhere to hide,
Dark of the nightfall, beautiful Dark!
Dark of the nightfall, beautiful Dark!

Beau—ootiful Daa—aark!
Beau—ootiful Daa—aark!
Darkness of Nightfall,
Beautiful, beautiful Dark!

Even in daylight thou seemst to say,
I'm in the shadows, come, come away.
Not long do we tarry, swift ends the day.
Dark of the nightfall, beautiful Dark!
Dark of the nightfall, beautiful Dark!
Beau—ootiful Daa—aark!
Beau—ootiful Daa—aark!
Darkness of Nightfall,
Beautiful, beautiful Dark!

Creep in about us, comforting gloom,
Without your predations, we'd run out of room,
We welcome you, welcome you, welcome you, doom.
Dark of the nightfall, beautiful Dark!
Dark of the nightfall, beautiful Dark!
Beau—ootiful Daa—aark!
Beau—ootiful Daa—aark!
Darkness of Nightfall,
Beautiful, beautiful Dark!

"Chorus again!" cried one of the voices, just as Julian found himself in absolute blackness. The branches stopped pushing. All the trees had just begun to repeat the chorus when a very different voice called out, "Time for the judging! He's needed for the judging!"

"Out, out, out, then!" said one of the tree voices while the rest continued to sing. Branches swept him forward again, but not, to Julian's dismay, back into the light. It was as dark as ever when the words faded into the distance:

Darkness of Nightfall,
Beautiful, beautiful Dark!

He realized, suddenly, that the branches were no longer urging him forward, though he'd kept on walking.

Julian stopped.

"You might go a little further," said a voice.

"Contrariwise, you might stop where you are," said a voice much like the first. "It hardly matters to us. *You* be the judge."

"He *is* the judge," said the first.

"I don't suppose," said Julian, "that you would have a light?"

"If you suppose we did, then we may not," said the first voice.

"Contrariwise," said the second, "if you supposed we didn't, we might yet. And if you didn't suppose at all, we could still. That's logic."

Suddenly, the sun was blazing overhead, and Julian found that he was standing on the edge of a cloud. If he only took a step to the left, he'd go plummeting toward the distant ground.

The speakers, not to Julian's surprise at all, turned out to be wearing identical outfits, and stood, each with an arm around the other's neck, a little higher up on the cloud. Julian could see 'DUM' embroidered on one of the collars, and 'DEE' on the other. Of course, round the back of each collar would be 'TWEEDLE.'

What did surprise Julian was that Tweedledum and Tweedledee were not fat. In fact, they were almost skeletal.

"Bring on the Ace!" said Tweedledum, and four playing cards entered through a door in the cloud. Two of the cards walked on either side of the Ace of Spades, who was struggling heroically against them.

The fourth card, walking behind, carried a large axe on his shoulder.

"I won't! I won't!" said the struggling Ace. "I positively refuse! Never! Never!"

"What's this about?" said Julian.

"It's about over," said Tweedledee.

The soldier cards dragged the struggling Ace behind a screen that was just short enough to show the axe rise a moment before it fell with a great CHOP!

Three cards emerged from behind the screen and exited.

"What do you think?" said Tweedledum.

"Ghastly!" Julian said.

"Quite," said Tweedledee.

"Contrariwise," said Tweedledum, "it was *heroic*. But is it the best?"

"The best?"

"That's right," said Tweedledee. "He's only seen one."

"The Deuce! The Deuce!" cried Tweedledum.

Four cards emerged from the door in the cloud. This time, the prisoner was the Deuce of Spades.

"He's not struggling," observed Julian.

"Why should I?" said the Deuce. "The thing to do is accept what's coming. There's nothing to be done, anyway."

The cards went behind the screen. The axe rose and fell with a CHOP!

As the surviving cards left, Tweedledum said, "Well?"

"Horrid!" Julian said.

"I was thinking *philosophical*," said Tweedledee.

"Better than the first?" asked his brother of Julian.

"You're asking me to *compare* them?"

"He's right," said Tweedledee. "He has to see them all before he can decide."

Next was the Trey of Spades. He giggled as he was led toward the screen.

"What's funny about this?" Julian said.

"It won't really happen, you know," the card said. "This is a big cosmic joke. What happens next is an illusion. Nobody really dies. I'll be right back, you'll see."

The axe rose and fell.

"*Foolish*," said Tweedledee. "There are some advantages to that one."

"They don't last long," observed Tweedledum. "Four's next." He called out, "The Four! The Four!"

The Four of Spades emerged and actually led the way to the screen. He tried to hold himself up, make himself a little taller than his guards. "I give myself willingly," he said. "Let there be a lesson in this. I permit, I invite it, so that you will all remember!"

"*Martyr's death*," Tweedledee said as the axe fell.

"Well I don't think I *will* forget it," Julian said, "or any of the others!"

"You can hardly call it outstanding, in that case," said Tweedledum, and he called for the Five.

The Five of Spades had to be dragged to the screen. He said nothing, looked at no one.

"*Morbid* sort," said Tweedledee a moment in advance of the CHOP!

"He has my sympathy," said Julian.

"But does he have your vote?" asked Tweedledum.

"Yes," said Tweedledee. "Which one wins?"

"I can hardly say that any of them won," said Julian.

"A tie!" said Tweedledum and Tweedledee together.

Tweedledum added, "Wonderful!"

"Blue ribbons for all of them!" said Tweedledee, clapping his bony hands. "How democratic!"

"Well done! Well done!"

"And since we are done," said Julian, "how do we get down?"

"Well," said Tweedledum, "you could jump."

Julian looked over the edge of the cloud. The ground was a very long way down. "Jump?" he said. "That would be suicide."

"Contrariwise," said Tweedledee, "it could be homicide, with the proper encouragement." And he gave Julian a push, then jumped behind him. Tweedledum followed.

As they fell, Tweedledum said, "Jumping is to Suicide as Pushing is to Homicide."

"How about burning?" said Tweedledee.

"Firecide," said Tweedledum.

"Drowning?"

"Lakecide!"

"Oceancide!"

"Rivercide!"

"Pondcide!"

"Poolcide!"

"Sewercide!"

"Oh, that one's especially good," said Tweedledum.

"Then there's dying in your sleep," said Tweedledee. "That's bedcide."

"In an automobile: Roadcide."

"By falling: cliffcide or mountaincide."

"It's not the falling that kills you," said Tweedledum. "It's the hasty stop at the end."

"Speaking of which," said Tweedledee, "how about leaping from a tall building?"

Tweedledum scratched his head with a skeletal finger. "Give me a hint?"

"What are you likely to meet?"

"The Cidewalk!"

Until then, Julian had been too busy falling to take part in the conversation, but he noticed that although they seemed to be dropping like stones, the ground was not getting any closer. "I wonder," he said, "if perhaps we'll survive."

"We have so far," said Tweedledum.

"Contrariwise," said Tweedledee, "that's not always the best indication." Then he said, "We haven't asked if you like poetry."

"Some poetry," Julian said cautiously. "When there's time for it and my mind isn't quite so occupied with death."

"That's the very time!" said Tweedledum. "What shall we repeat to him? We barely have time for one before we hit, I think."

"'*The Tiger and the Engineer*' is the longest," Tweedledee replied. "If we have time for just one, we should make it a long one." And he began to recite.

> The void was empty as a pail
> Containing only air:
> Except the air was absent and
> The pail, it wasn't there.
> How long this lasted none could say
> As none was quite aware.

The absence finally ceased to be,
It simply couldn't last,
When Something suddenly arrived
From nowhere with no past.
No one was there to measure it,
But it was Something vast.

The stars bunched into galaxies,
The land cooled and congealed;
The sun shone bright and tartly
Like a lemon that's been peeled,
When two came walking close at hand
Across the cosmic field.

The Tiger and the Engineer,
Who trod the new-made ground,
Saw absence in the Somethingness:
"There's still not much around!"
They said, "If there were more to this,
We'd find it more profound."

The Engineer, whose task it was
To supplement Creation,
Began to work, though at his back,
With equal application,
The Tiger stalked to bring his works
To their annihilation.

Said he, "We need some mountains
To enhance the flat horizon."
The Tiger said she quite agreed,
So Engineer devised 'em.
Then with her massive sweeping tail
The Tiger pulverized 'em.

"And if there were some trees about,
Now wouldn't that be grand?"
So Engineer arranged for some
To sprout out of the sand.
The Tiger gave each trunk a swat
That no tree could withstand.

Then for a while the Tiger walked
Most peaceably behind,
While Engineer was raising up
Two things of every kind,
From fish to frogs to chimpanzees,
And then, at last, mankind.

The Earthly population swelled;
The Tiger was astounded.
"And now we'll dance a merry dance,"
The Engineer expounded,
"To celebrate fecundity
And all that we have founded."

Hand in paw and paw in hand
They circled as they sang,
"Not long ago was nothing,
Now we've got the whole shebang,
From shoes and ships and sealing wax
To Finland and meringue!"

"The time has come," the Tiger said,
"To focus our attention
On how this crowd will grow and grow
Without some intervention."
The Engineer considered this
With growing apprehension.

"Why not let them multiply
And swell and grow forever?
These recent ones, the hairless apes
Are marvelously clever.
They'll entertain us endlessly:
Just see how they endeavor!"

And it was true, these human things
Were good at clever tricks.
They dressed themselves in ostrich skins,
Built Taj Mahals with bricks;
They learned to ski and parachute
And light cigars with Bics.

"I'm tempted some," the Tiger said,
"To do as you suggest,
And let them cover all the globe,
Key Largo to Trieste.
The counter argument is this:
They're easy to digest."

With her great paw, the Tiger snatched
A recent generation,
Chewed it up and swallowed it,
And said with some elation,
"With claw and tooth I engineer
Creation's cancellation."

Just what she meant to say by that
Was in a moment clear,
For in a gulp she ate the anti-
Podal hemisphere.
She ate the ground they stood upon;
She ate the Engineer.

When she had swallowed all the Earth,
She took a bite of Mars,
And when she finished chewing that
She swallowed up the stars.
The Tiger then was singular,
Which briefly felt bizarre.

"A Tiger ought to finish what
A Tiger starts to do,"
That's what she said, and bit her tail,
And ate herself up, too.
Thus begins a Universe,
And thus it bids adieu.

On that last word, Tweedledee disappeared, and with him, Tweedledum. In their place was a man in black armor. He wore a helmet in the shape of a horse's head, and in his arms was a large bundle of rags.

"Well, here I am, to the rescue," he said.

"What's that?" said Julian, nodding at the bundle. "A parachute?"

"Perhaps rescue was the wrong word," said the Black Knight. "What I should have said is, 'Here I am, reliably.'"

"Oh," said Julian. "So that's who you are."

As they fell, the wind began to unwind the rags, which weren't rags, really, but one piece of cloth. A shroud.

"Tell me," said Julian. "Tell me why."

"*Lots* of reasons," said the Knight. "There are poems and songs about it. *You* should know."

"I want your opinion," Julian said. "I want your version."

"Well," said the Knight, "there is a song that I'm particularly fond of. If you'd like to hear it."

"I asked, didn't I?"

"So you did," said the Knight. And he sang:

I met a sickly, sickly man
Upon his bed a-lying:
I tapped him with a two-by-four
And asked why he was dying.
"See here," I said, "I want to know
What is your soul's intention?"
I asked because it mattered, though
I failed to pay attention.

He said, "I die because the whales
Who swim the salty waters
Won't introduce me to their wives,
Much less unto their daughters.
And so I die of loneliness
for love I never knew,
The floaty whale-ish sort of love
That might my life renew."

But I was thinking of a plan
To dig a hole so deep
Insomniacs could hurtle down
And safely fall asleep.
This hole would open at each end,
A metaphor for living.
Distracted thus, I had to shout,
"What answer were you giving?"

He coughed a bit, and then he wheezed,
"I'll tell you if I must,
The likes of me is never pleased
To linger here as dust.
I'm meant for finer things, you know,
I'm made in God's own image.
I'll live on as a concept, say,
A quark or line of scrimmage."

But I was puzzling out a means
Of earning higher wages
By building artificial Queens
For London's daily pages.
"See here!" I said, "You make me feel
I'm wasting all my breath!
Now tell me how it is you die,
And why life ends in death!"

He said, "The answer's plain enough,
You needn't holler so.
I'll tell you how it is we come
And why we have to go.
Life is a rope of broken pearls
That once was painted green,
It's carried by a pair of girls
Who stop sometimes to preen.

"The butter that they walk upon
Spews from eternal churns,
The pearls glow like the pages
Of a novel as it burns.
And so, you see, simplicity
Requires that our lot
Be that we exit, when we must,
With only what we brought."

For once I followed what he said,
Since I had finished thinking
About a poison that would cure
The ills of too much drinking.
I thanked him much for telling me
His insights into dying.
He said it was a piece of cake,
Then did it without trying.

"I suppose," Julian said, "that's as satisfactory an answer as I'm going to hear."

"I haven't heard any better," said the Knight, "and I've heard them all, believe me." The blowing shroud knocked his helmet slightly askew, but he didn't rearrange it. "Any time you're ready," said the Knight, "you can reach out and grab my hand."

"And if I'm not ready?"

"Then sooner or later," said the Knight, "I'll reach out and grab yours."

The shroud continued to unwind and at last ripped free in the wind. Anna's body, curled up like a baby's, rested in the Black Knight's arms; the fingers of his right hand twined with hers.

Julian reached out to stroke Anna's hair and tuck a flying strand behind her ear. He thought of the end of a different poem, a poem about another woman dying. He'd heard the first lines of it just recently. In ended like this:

We waited while She passed –
It was a narrow time –
Too jostled were Our Souls to speak
At length the notice came.

She mentioned, and forgot –
Then lightly as a Reed
Bent to the Water, struggled scarce –
Consented, and was dead –

And We — We placed the Hair –
And drew the Head erect –
And then an awful leisure was
Belief to regulate –

"That's a good one, too," said the Black Knight. Julian hadn't known he was speaking the lines aloud.

"Contrariwise," said Julian, "they're all good. It's not a question of which poems to say. It's a question of saying enough of them enough times."

The Knight was silent for a bit and then said, "I'm not sure I follow you."

"I didn't ask you to, did I?" said Julian.

"Didn't ask me to what?" said Anna's mother. She had gotten up to tuck a strand of Anna's hair into place, then returned to her chair next to Yvonne.

Julian's leg tingled. It was falling asleep. He shifted Nick on his lap and said, "For something to drink," Julian said. "How about some juice? Nick, that sound good to you?"

Nick nodded with his whole body, head and shoulders going in opposite directions. "Apple juice!"

"Yvonne?"

His daughter sat very still in her chair, looking at her mother's lifeless face. She had known that her mother was dying. It had been explained to her many times. But it was clear that she didn't know what to do with the event now that it had arrived. She hadn't cried. She hadn't asked any questions.

"Yvonne? Some juice?"

"Okay," she said.

Anna's mother left the viewing room.

Julian took his daughter's hand in his. She didn't respond. Julian followed her gaze to the place where Anna lay.

Julian squeezed Yvonne's hand and sang a single note three times: "Mi, mi, mi."

Yvonne kept staring straight ahead. Julian withdrew his hand, bounced Nick on his knee and sang,

Ring around the rosie,
Pockets full of posy,
Ashes, ashes,
We all fall down!

Yvonne looked at him. Julian started the song over, and Nick struggled to get out of his lap. Julian set him down.

"Ashes, ashes," Julian sang, and Nick started to dance. He collapsed on cue, then said, "Do it again!"

"And again and again," Julian promised. And to his daughter, he said, "If you want to, you can help me sing."

Nick sang, "Rosie, rosie!"

Yvonne smiled a little, then stopped smiling.

"If you want," Julian said.

And then he repeated the song, singing it as if it were the song that Nick thought it was, a song about playing on the grass in a circle. But Yvonne was old enough, knew enough now, that she might be able to hear what was really in the words. It was in the words of so many songs. But not enough. New songs were needed all the time, and they needed singing again and again.

You've got to go deeper in, Julian thought, to get further out.

"Ashes, ashes," he sang, "We all fall down."

And on the next verse, his daughter joined in.

Introduction to "The Brass Man Who Would Sink"

In the heyday of pulp fiction, some contributors to the various magazines were so prolific that they might have three or four stories in the same issue. The editors disguised such frequent contributors with fake bylines so that readers wouldn't know that one writer had written half of the contents. The editors who bought "Heart of Shanodin" wanted to use "The Brass Man Who Would Sink" in the same anthology, so this story first appeared under the byline of Hanovi Braddock.

The Brass Man Who Would Sink

In olden times, when the sun was whiter and the stars were brighter and but one moon hung in the sky, there lived a miller whose son was as handsome as his mother was poor. And poor the miller was indeed, for the stream that drove her mill had little by little and year by year dried up. Now it was only a trickle, and far from the flow needed to turn the great grinding wheel. The miller's neighbors carted their harvest far away to have it milled. The miller grew so poor that soon all that was left to her were the mill and the cherry tree behind it.

Though she was poor, the miller wanted the best for her son. Only a rich suitor would do for him. When a farm girl came courting with her family and a bouquet of wildflowers, the miller and her husband drove them off.

"But mother, I know of her," said the miller's son, picking up the flowers the young woman had dropped. "All say she has an honest heart, a quick mind, and a gentle hand. With her I might know the Delight of Two Hearts." For he was a pious lad, and the Delights of the Prophets were more in his mind than were any thoughts of riches.

But the miller would not be moved. Her son would live in a rich house, not some farm house. Her husband was not quite so sure. There was much to be said for the Delight of Two

Hearts. Had not he and the miller found such happiness? But though he had some say in the matter, her word was final.

One day, as the miller's husband was walking home from the forest with a load of wood on his back, he met a party of hunters. Among them were the lady of the nearby lands and an even more richly dressed woman whom the miller had never before seen.

"Cutting wood. There's a labor I'm happy never to have done," said the lady, making a sour face.

"Would that I never had to do it again, madam," said the miller's husband. "I must cut wood these days to earn our bread. I'd give anything to be free of such toil."

"You're the miller's husband, are you not? Do you speak with the voice of your household? If you mean what you say, I can see to it that you need never labor so again. I'll exchange these rings on my fingers and a heavy bag of gold for what's behind your mill."

What could the lady mean but the cherry tree? The miller's husband eagerly agreed, the bargain was written and signed, and the lady dropped her heavy gold rings with their heavy great jewels, *plop, plop, plop* into the husband's hands.

To the husband, the lady said, "In a month, I'll bring the gold and come for what's mine." Then to the richly dressed stranger, she added, "Justiciar, you have born witness."

"I have," said the justiciar, adjusting her robes, "and the weight of the law seals this bargain."

The husband arrived home rejoicing, and the miller sang out in delight when she saw the rings with their great gems. "But what did you give in the exchange?" she said.

"The lady asked only for what's behind our mill. That cherry tree is certainly something we can do without!"

The miller laughed. "What would she want with a cherry tree? Husband, she can't have meant that! Our son was behind the mill, airing out the bedclothes."

The husband went white with this news.

"Come, come," said the miller. "It's a good bargain after all. Our son will live a rich life as the lady's consort. "We've provided for him well."

"For his body, perhaps, but not for his heart," said the husband, who knew his son.

He was right. The son, upon hearing the news that he would be a lady's keepling, flew into a rage. He stormed out of the mill house and into the forest, and none of his father's commands or entreaties would bring him back.

The son marched deep into the forest, and then deeper still, further than he had ever gone before. At last he came to a clearing where there sat a pile of stones and a great clump of bushes. The young man was tired of walking by then but he was still full of fury. One by one, he picked up the stones and hurled them at the bushes.

Whoosh! went the first stone as it scattered green leaves. *Whoosh!* went the second. *Clang!* went the third.

Now there's a mystery, the young man thought, and curiosity overcame his anger. He parted the branches of the bushes, and what should he find but a man of brass? The metal figure stood at attention like a soldier, and had stood so long that it was sinking into the earth. Everything below the knees was already under ground.

"A little enchantment might make a great warrior of you," the young man said, "but I don't see what use a warrior is to me." And he walked slowly homeward, his anger spent, but his sorrow enduring.

He did not come out of the forest quite the same way that he'd gone in, so found himself crossing ground he'd never walked before. As night fell, he lost his way, but he saw a little square of yellow light and made for it. It was the window of a woodswoman's hut. I'll ask directions here, he thought, and he opened the door.

Inside was a very, very old woman, whose head bobbed constantly up and down and whose hands shook like leaves in the wind. She was tending a fire that did not smoke.

"Many pardons," the young man said. "Do you know the way to the mill house?"

"The mill house?" said the old woman. "The family that turned my granddaughter out when she came courting?"

"The same," the young man said. "But refusing your granddaughter was no wish of mine." And he told her the story of how he'd been pledged against his desires.

"You poor child," she said. "The lady of these lands keeps her consorts brightly jeweled and richly dressed, but before long their hearts turn to ice and they die."

"What can I do?" he asked her. "If I run away, I'll be a pledge thief and outlaw."

"Think on this riddle," said the old woman. "What is yours that you might not give whole? When you have the answer, give a measure to my granddaughter and to her alone. From this very moment speak no word to anyone before you have done this." Then she took up a knife, reached into the unsmoking fire, and snipped off a little flame as if it were a bit of wool from a sheep's haunch. The old woman put the flame in a tinder box, put the tinder box into a bread basket, and put the basket under her cot. Only then did she point the way to the mill.

The miller's son nodded his thanks and departed. He spoke no word during the days that followed, which his father took as a sign of grief and his mother as a sign of stubbornness. But all the while his thoughts were on the riddle.

When the time was up and the lady arrived with her bag of gold, her huntsmen and the justiciar came with her. No sooner had they appeared at the miller's door than the farm girl, with her brothers and father and mother, also came into the miller's yard. "We've a stake in this matter," said the girl's mother, "for we made a prior suit which was not answered."

"Not answered!" said the miller. "Why I drove you from this very ground."

"Before you heard our suit," said the farmer. And her daughter added, "If we made any suit, let your son now repeat the terms of it."

But the miller's son was silent. He still puzzled over the riddle.

"A suit not heard is a suit not refused," said the justiciar. "It is no prior claim, but they've a right to be heard now. So stands the weight of the law."

"Well, let them say what they will," said the lady. "It's a small matter. I have a signed contract."

"A contract for what stands behind the mill, and what stands there now is a cherry tree," said the farm girl.

"The contract's well understood," said the lady, "or why are we arguing?"

"Not clear, not clear," said the justiciar, clicking her tongue. "A vague contract might not hold. So stands the weight of the law."

"But you, Justiciar, were witness!" said the lady. And then she threw the bag of gold at the miller's feet, hoping this would seal the matter. "Miller, is that not the gold as promised?"

The miller hefted the bag and smiled. But her husband took the bag from her, and though it was indeed heavy, he shook it as if it were a bag of eggshells. "Not so heavy as I thought was promised," he said.

The miller glared at him. "Heavy enough," she said, taking the bag again. "He's my son, so it's my judgment that matters."

"But the contract was agreed by his father," said the farm girl.

"Tis so, tis so," said the justiciar.

The miller and the lady both glared at the justiciar. "Do you mean to say that this contract would not stand?"

"Well," said the justiciar, and she leaned one way and told one side of the question. Then she leaned the other way and told the other side, as lawyers are wont to do. In the end, her answer said nothing at all.

"The law is slow and uncertain," said the farm girl. "Let us agree to some other test of the contract."

The lady smiled at this. "Fine, fine," she said. "Yon wheatfield is in need of harvesting. If all the wheat is cut and sheaved by dawn tomorrow, the contract shall be void. But if there is the smallest scratch or blister on the young man's hands, he shall be mine."

With that she reclaimed her bag of gold and rode off, with her huntsmen and the justiciar close behind. The miller was so angry that she marched into the mill house without a word, husband at her heels. The farm girl's family started away, too, but the girl herself lingered for a moment.

"Have you anything to say to me?" she asked the miller's son.

"Memory is mine, but I might not give it whole," he said, for he had solved the riddle. "Here is a thing I remember—deep in the forest is a clearing. In the center and overgrown with bushes stands a brass man so ancient that he sinks into the ground."

"Well answered," said the farm girl. "You must meet me in that place by moonlight, but touch no tool and do no work before then."

The miller's son did as she said. When the moon was high, he met her in the clearing where the brass man was. The farm girl chopped down the bushes and dug free the brass man's legs and feet. Then she opened a tinder box and out jumped the flame of the unsmoking fire. She spoke a word to the flame, and the fire went out as the brass man opened his eyes.

"Command him," said the farm girl. So the miller's son told the brass man to harvest the wheat. The brass man was off quick as lightning, and by the time the miller's son and farmer's daughter had found their way out of the woods, the sky was just growing light in the east and every stalk of wheat was cut and sheaf bound up.

The brass man, who had done all the work with his metal hands, now bowed before them. A sparrow lighted on his shoulder and said, "*Cheap, cheap, cheap!* Though I've served queens and wizards well, I'll not find rest 'til I find hell, so let me sink." Then the brass man's head nodded, his eyes closed, and the sparrow flew away.

"We should release him," said the miller's son. "He has served us well."

"Not yet," said the farmer's daughter, and she covered the brass man with branches to hide him.

When the lady, her huntsman and the justiciar returned, they were quite surprised to see the wheat all cut and bound into sheaves, but what surprised them even more was the condition of the young man's hands. There was no scratch, nor blister, nor even blemish upon them. The miller herself was no less amazed.

"Let me see again," the lady insisted, and this time when the miller's son held out his hands, she marked the palm of his hand with a pin. "I see a scratch," she said.

"Where none was before!" said the miller's son.

"A scratch is a scratch," said the miller, eyeing the bag of gold.

"Justiciar?" said the lady.

Once again, the justiciar leaned to the left and considered the matter in one view, then leaned to the right and considered it another way.

"Enough!" said the lady. "We'll settle it thus: The wheat needs to be threshed. If he brings in all the sheaves and threshes the grain before tomorrow morning, then the contract shall be void. But if there is any fleck of chaff or straw upon him, then the young man is mine." With that, she clutched her bag of gold and rode off with her huntsmen and the justiciar. As before, the miller was so upset that she went into her house without a word, and her husband went close behind her.

"Touch no stalk of straw, but meet me by moonlight where we left the brass man," said the farm girl.

The miller's son did as she said. When the moon was high, he found her already removing the branches that hid the brass man. To the young man's surprise, the brass man had sunk into the soft earth a little ways, so that the farm girl had to dig free his ankles. Then she opened her tinder box and out jumped the flame of unsmoking fire. She spoke the word, the flame went out, and the brass man opened his eyes.

"Command him," said the farm girl. So the miller's son told the brass man to bring in the sheaves and thresh them. "And winnow as well," said the farm girl. The brass man was off in a glint of moonlight. Almost faster than the eye could follow, he carried the sheaves to the mill house, threshed the seed from the stalks with his metal hands, and tossed the seed into the night breeze to winnow it. He stacked the straw as well. By the time the sky was turning pink in the east, the miller's yard was covered by a great mound of finished grain, a breeze-blown carpet of chaff, and a haystack.

The brass man now bowed before them. A robin lighted on his shoulder and said, "*Cheeryup! Cheeryup! Chereep!* Though I've served queens and wizards well, I'll not find rest 'til I find hell, so let me sink." Then the brass man's head nodded, his eyes closed, and the robin flew away.

"Truly, we should do as he asks," said the miller's son. "He has served us well."

"Not yet," said the farmer's daughter, and she again hid the brass man with branches.

Imagine the surprise of the lady, her huntsman and the justiciar when they returned. Not only was the grain threshed, but winnowed, too! The lady dismounted and sifted the grain in her hands, and it was clean. She sifted the chaff, and there was no grain in it. Even more amazingly, there was no speck of chaff on the young man's clothes, no sliver of straw in his hair. The miller, too, was amazed.

"Let me see again," the lady insisted, and this time when the miller's son bowed his head before her, she flicked a bit of chaff from her fingers into his hair. "I see chaff," she said.

"Where none was before!" said the miller's son.

"Chaff is chaff," said the miller, looking at the lady's saddlebags where the bag of gold must be.

"Justiciar?" said the lady.

Once again, the justiciar leaned to the left and considered the matter in one view, then leaned to the right and considered it another way.

"Enough!" said the lady. She put her hands on her hips, and she looked high and low. At last she spied the stream with its meager trickle, too little to drive the grinding wheel. "We'll settle it thus: The grain must be milled. If he makes flour of all this wheat before tomorrow morning, then the contract shall be void. But if there is any trace of dust or flour upon him, then the young man is mine." With that, she climbed into her saddle and rode off with her huntsmen and the justiciar. As they went, she leaned toward one of her huntsmen and said, "There's more to this than we know." So that huntsman rode into the woods and hid himself to see what he might see.

The miller was again upset, but this time she stayed in the yard. "Are you mad?" she asked her son. "Here a fine lady will have you, and you'll not be hers?"

So her son told her what he knew of the lady, that the lady kept her consorts brightly jeweled and richly dressed. "But before long, mother, their hearts turn to ice and they die."

Now at last the miller understood, but she feared it was too late. "The stream will never drive the grinding wheel," she said. "My son, my son, you are lost!"

"Not so," said the farm girl. And she told the miller's son to bathe and to wash his clothes, so that there would be no trace of dust upon him to begin with. "Then meet me by moonlight again," she said.

The miller's son did as she said. When the moon was high, he helped her to remove the branches that hid the brass man. This time the brass man had sunk into the soft earth half the distance to his knees, so that the farm girl had to dig him free again. Then she opened her tinder box and out jumped the flame of unsmoking fire. She spoke the word, the flame went out, and the brass man opened his eyes.

"Command him," said the farm girl. So the miller's son told the brass man to grind the wheat into flour. "And put it into bags as well," said the farm girl. The brass man did not even go inside the mill, but did all the grinding with his metal hands and let the flour fall into bags. The farm girl tied the bags when they were full, but the miller's son stayed well away, so that he'd not be dusted with the flour. By the time the first cock was crowing, the miller's yard was stacked with bags of flour.

The brass man bowed before them. A kestrel lighted on his shoulder and said, "*Killy, killy, killy!* Though I've served queens and wizards well, I'll not find rest 'til I find hell, so let me sink." Then the brass man's head nodded, his eyes closed, and the bright-feathered kestrel flew away.

"Let us do as he asks," said the miller's son. "Has he not served us well?"

"Not quite yet," said the farmer's daughter, and she again hid the brass man with branches.

Now all this was seen by the huntsman who had stayed behind, and he rode forth to meet the lady as she approached with the rest of the huntsmen and the justiciar. The lady smiled when she heard what the huntsman had to say. She ordered him to return to her estate to bring the carriage.

In the miller's yard, the lady made a great show of carefully inspecting the quality of each bag's flour. She sifted it with her fingers. When the miller's son stepped forward for the justiciar to see that there was no trace of dust upon him, he was careful not to let the lady dust him with her floury fingers. But the lady did not even try. Instead she said, "The bargain was that the young man would harvest the sheaves, thresh the grain, and grind the flour. But he has not done so. A brass man has done it all!"

"By my command, it was done," said the young man. "If you command your tenants to build a road, do you not say that the road was your doing?"

The justiciar cleared her throat and began to lean first one way in her saddle, but the lady waved at her impatiently. "I don't care about the finer points!" she said. "I made an agreement, and I was tricked!" She flung her bag of gold at the miller's feet.

"No," said the miller. "I don't consent. Take back your gold."

"Too late," said the lady. "Your word was given and the young man was pledged to me. What's more, I'm claiming the means by which you have tricked me. The brass man is mine as well."

Just then, the huntsman drove up with the carriage and pointed out for his lady the place where the brass man was hidden. The brass man had already sunk as far as his ankles again, so that the huntsmen had to dig him out before they could load him into the carriage.

"I tell you," said the miller, "there is no bargain for my son."

"And I tell you that I am a lady, mistress of a great house. You are only a miller."

"Well, before the law—"

"Shut up, Justiciar," the lady said. She told her huntsmen to draw their long hunting knives so that no one should stop what she next commanded. She had the miller's son tied hand and foot and thrown over her saddle like a great bag of flour, and her horse was tied behind the carriage. The carriage set out then, with the brass man and the lady riding inside.

When the huntsmen put away their knives and rode off, the farm girl ran after the carriage. She ran until her breath burned in her chest, but she could not keep the carriage in sight. Still she ran. Even as her heart might burst, she ran, but the carriage went on and on.

The miller's son, on the back of the lady's horse, was half dead with despair. When he heard the rush of wings sweeping past him, he did not even raise his head until the third time.

A crow circled the carriage and the horse. At last the great black bird settled on the roof of the carriage, and it called, "*Caw, caw, caw!* Though I've served queens and wizards well, I'll not find rest 'til I find hell, so let me sink." Then the crow flew away.

Now the young man had troubles of his own to worry about, so he did not say anything at first. But as the carriage was passing a graveyard, he said in a loud voice, "Brass man, though you saved me not you served me well, so let you find your rest in hell. Now may you sink."

At that, the wheels of the carriage began to rattle and slow. The carriage grew so heavy that the horses could no longer pull it, though the huntsman in the driver's seat whipped them furiously.

When the ground began to shake, the horse carrying the young man reared and threw him to the ground.

The carriage axles strained and broke. The road cracked open, and the whole carriage, with the brass man, the lady, the huntsman driver, the team of horses before and the lady's horse behind, all sank into the depths of the earth. The remaining huntsmen fled in terror. The ground closed again, and only the justiciar on her horse and the miller's son remained.

The justiciar cleared her throat. "When one party to a bargain is swallowed up by the earth," she said, "the contract is undone. So stands the weight of the law." Then she turned her horse and slowly rode away.

It is said that the farm girl found the miller's son sitting in the middle of the road, wriggling out of the ropes that had bound him. It is further said that they were soon married and lived their lives in the Delight of Two Hearts.

And that, any woman of the law can tell you, is hearsay. You might lean one way in your saddle and consider it a lie. You might lean the other, and say that it is so.

Introduction to "Ever So Much"

Dogs sometimes appear in fantasy stories, mysteries, or fairy tales, but cats dominate. Of course. It's not hard to imagine a cat who has a secret, or a secret power. But a mysterious dog? A magical dog? No, if you want clever plots, intrigue, and dead wildlife hidden in your shoes for discovery at a later date, you want a cat.

Ever So Much

I

Once upon a time in a fishing village along the windy shore there lived a boy with neither mother nor father. His name was Duncan, but the villagers called him Small Catch, which described his usual haul. When he might have been mending his nets in his tiny hut, he was as likely to be gazing into the fire while thinking of the grand palaces of kings. When he was out upon the sea, he watched the horizon and dreamed of distant shores and other countries, forgetting to lower his nets until half the day was gone. Even on his best days, he caught hardly enough to feed himself.

Duncan's boat leaked. One day, as he was pounding bits of old rope into the very worst gaps, he looked up to see one of the village men striding over the rocks toward the sea with a burlap sack in his hand. Something inside the sack squirmed and mewled. Duncan put down his mallet and followed the man. "What do you have there?"

The man stopped and looked at Duncan. Then he held up the sack. "A wee cat," he said. "Runt of the litter, and bound to die anyway."

"Ah," Duncan said, for he understood that the man mean to throw sack and all into the sea. "Will you let me have it, then?"

The man considered a moment, then laughed. "Aye, by rights the runt *should* belong to Small Catch." And that is how Duncan came to own a cat.

II

From then on, Duncan's fishing was worse than ever. To any other villager, a kitten was useless until it was a cat, and as a cat it was good for nothing more than catching rats. But Duncan took great pleasure in playing with his kitten as it grew up, and just as much pleasure in watching it when it was grown, even though the cat—like most cats—spent much of its day sleeping. Duncan took to the sea just often enough to see that he and his cat did not starve, and it was a near thing at that. Some days he caught only one silverling. Other days he landed only a pin fish, which he had to prepare carefully to avoid the poison in its liver.

A kind of loyalty passed between the boy and his cat, though it was hard to say whether it was the cat that was loyal to Duncan or the other way around. They were always together except when Duncan put out to sea. On the narrow village paths or along the rocky shore, the cat followed Duncan or Duncan followed the cat. Villagers joked that it was a good match, that each was as industrious as the other.

On one rare sunny day, Duncan sat with his cat among the rocks. Duncan was on one side of a tide pool, and the cat was on the other side. Duncan watched the light glittering on the sea, then closed his eyes. He sighed. "Oh, my little cat," he said. "What is to become of me? The thing that I do best is dream, but there is no fortune in dreaming."

A high, little voice, just like a cat's voice, said, "There is ever so much to see."

Duncan opened his eyes wide and looked at his cat. The cat calmly returned his gaze. Duncan looked to the left and to the right. He looked behind. No one else was near. "Little cat, little cat!" he said. "What did you say?"

But the cat only peered down into the tide pool, as if it knew full well that Duncan had heard and remembered the words. Duncan peered into the pool, too. At first he saw only water, rocks, and sand. Then he noticed the tiny motions of an itsy bitsy crab creeping along a crack. He saw a minnow dart from one shadow to another. The longer he watched, the more he saw. An urchin waved the little arms that grew between its spines. A starfish crossed the sandy bottom no faster than the sun crosses the sky.

This was not the first time that Duncan had stared into a tide pool. This was not the first time that he had noticed more and more tiny creatures the longer he looked. But this was the first time that he had taken into his heart the truth that there was, indeed, ever so much to see. And not only in the pool, but on the rocks, along the shoreline, in the bird-filled air above and the in the clouds far beyond, there was ever so much to see.

III

Now Duncan the dreamer was Duncan the watcher as well. He was yet more idle than before, for when he would begin to mend his nets he would notice how each knot had its own shape, how captured bits of kelp were of different kinds, how the salt drifted from net to the earthen floor, dusting it white. Like his cat, he would sit for a long time with his eyes half-closed, considering the wood grain in the walls of his hut.

One day when all of the other boats were out but Duncan sat on the rocks watching the waves with his cat, a great procession of men and horses came along the shore. Duncan and the cat watched them, and there was ever so much to see. In advance of the procession rode two helmeted soldiers wearing the king's colors of red and gold. They scowled at Duncan as they drew near. Then came a boy no older than Duncan, dressed in silken leggings and a quilted tunic. His face was pale, his arms were thin, and he seemed barely able to hold himself erect in the saddle. A red-bearded man dressed much the same rode close beside him, as if to catch the boy if he fell. Behind these came two worried looking men dressed in black. The thin one clutched a holy book, gazed heavenward, and moved his lips in prayer. The fat one glanced warily at the surf that lapped the horses' hooves and at the waves farther out from shore, as if he did not trust the sea to stay in its place. Behind these came solemn men in the quilted, ruffed, and silken clothes of court, followed by more soldiers. There was ever so much to see!

Duncan scrambled over the rocks, cat following behind him, to keep up and to see what more there might be to see. So he was near enough to see the pale boy's head loll with sleepiness. He was near enough to see the red-bearded man shake the boy as if to wake him and keep him in the saddle. And Duncan was near enough to see something golden fall from the boy's hand and into a crack in the rocks, just before the boy himself toppled and landed in a heap on the sand.

The fat man in black urged his horse forward, dismounted, and unstopped phial that he held beneath the boy's nose. The thin man in black prayed all the harder. The rest of the procession waited. At last the physician had roused the boy, who was helped back into his saddle. The boy's hands trembled as he tried to hold the reins, but he smiled bravely as he spoke to those around him. Duncan felt sorry for him and also admired his determination.

The riders continued. Duncan raised his hand to wave "Ahoy!" to a soldier, but the soldier touched the hilt of his sword and glowered so darkly that Duncan dared not tell him that the boy had dropped something. Duncan waited. When the procession was gone from sight, he sought the fallen treasure.

"A box," he said, showing it to the cat. The outside was beaten gold, decorated with the shapes of birds and flowers. But when Duncan opened it, and saw the pages, he realized that it wasn't a box at all. It was a little book. Priests and learned men could read these words. "I wonder what it says?"

IV

The king's messengers brought word to all the villages on the coast that the prince, who had recently taken the sea air, had lost a treasured possession—a little golden book. Whoever presented himself at court with the book would receive a reward befitting the prince's gratitude. The whole village, from children to fathers to grandmothers were soon searching the shoreline for the prince's book. Duncan sat next to his overturned boat and watched them, feeling uneasy. His cat lay on top of the boat, eyes closed. Nearby, two young men of the village leaned against their own boats to watch the searchers.

"Oh, my little cat," Duncan said, "shall I tell them that they search in vain?"

A high little voice, just like a cat's voice, answered him: "There is ever so much to hear."

Duncan turned to look at his cat, but the cat's eyes were closed. "Little cat, little cat, what did you say?"

The cat opened its eyes, then stretched and yawned a yawn from the end of its tail to the tip of its tongue. It sat, closed its eyes again, and twitched its ears. It listened. Duncan closed his eyes, too. He heard the rush of the surf, the crying of gulls, the voices of children as they searched and called to their searching parents. Wind rolled in Duncan's ears. The more he listened, the more he heard. And though the two young men were some distance from him, he heard a boat creak as one of them leaned against it, and he heard the man say to his companion, "And why aren't you looking for it?"

"Because I've seen gulls snatching fish from other birds. It takes one kind to catch a fish, and another kind to eat it," the other man said. Then they both laughed. Whether this man was in earnest or not Duncan knew that what he said of gulls was true. Some gulls and some men found it easier to steal from others than to seek their own fortune. As soon as word got out that the prince's book had been found, no road between the village and the palace would be safe.

Duncan went inside his hut, wrapped some dried fish in a cloth, hid the golden book beneath his hat, and set out for the palace. His cat followed along. Every so often, they stopped by the side of the road to listen. When they drew near to the palace, Duncan heard a horse nicker softly in the woods where he thought no horse should be. He and the cat waited for nightfall, and then for midnight, and then for the moon to go down. Then they heard the conversations of a band of robbers who built a fire and cooked their dinner only now, when it was too dark for anyone to travel. Only then, when the robbers' thoughts were on the stewpot and their eyes were on the fire, did Duncan and his cat creep by in the dark.

V

Morning found them outside the palace. Duncan presented himself at the gate to claim his reward, and the cat darted in ahead of him, as cats will sometimes do at an open door. Where the cat had gone, Duncan did not know. Meanwhile, soldiers ushered Duncan into the throne room where the aged king sat on his throne and the ailing prince lay upon a litter. Beside the prince stood the priest, the physician, and the man with the red beard, who seemed not at all pleased to see so low a commoner in court. The prince, however, seemed not to notice the ragged state of Duncan's clothes. He was delighted to have his book returned to him. It was a book of poems, and he read one aloud before clutching the little book to his breast.

"Name your reward," said the prince, "and as it is in my power to grant, you shall have it."

And the king, who was pleased to see his ailing son so happy, added, "And as it is in *my* power, you shall have it."

Duncan looked at the high ceiling, the tapestries on the walls, the courtiers in their fine clothes. "I have often dreamed of being inside a palace," he said. "I ask for my reward only that I be permitted to stay a while at court."

"So shall it be," said the old king. To the red-bearded man, he said, "Brother, see to it that he is made suitable."

"My king," the man said, "I do not wish to leave my prince's side."

"I thank you for your devotion," the king said, "but you serve your nephew best by making this boy fit to be among us for a while."

The red-bearded man bowed, then he bade two guards and Duncan to follow him. As soon as they were out of the throne room, the king's brother said a word and the guards seized Duncan by the elbows and hurried him so brusquely through the halls that he thought surely they meant him harm. Even at a time such as this, Duncan remembered that there was ever so much to hear. The guards' boots clomped and echoed in the long hallways. Pots rattled and knives chopped, so that Duncan knew they were taking him to the kitchen even before the door was opened to the warmth and cooking smells. The king's brother dismissed the guards and summoned the cook. "Wash this," he said, waving his hand at Duncan. "It is to be made presentable at court."

"Him?" said the cook. "Him at court? Better to have one of my pots-and-pan boys before the king!"

"Indeed. But His Royal Highness commands it. Clothes will be sent. Burn the rags he's wearing." Then as he turned to go the king's brother muttered softly to himself, "No such follies when *I* am king."

There was ever so much for Duncan to hear.

"Right, then," said the cook. She called to her kitchen boys to bring a cauldron and water both hot and cold. "Clean him up," she commanded, "and don't spare the scouring brush out of kindness!" The boys made a bath of the cauldron, and they peeled and scrubbed Duncan as if he were a turnip. They kneaded him dry with rough towels and dressed him in the clothes that were brought.

Duncan's skin was sore, and the clothes itched against his skin, but when he was led up to the dining hall and saw the feast, he was glad that he had asked for this reward. There was ever so much to see: the honeyed meats, the fruits, the breads, the pastries. There was ever so much to hear: the worried conversations of the court, the tunes of the royal musicians. Duncan watched and listened and kept his peace. He learned how the courtiers feared for the prince's life. No effort had been spared for him. His priest was the holiest of men. The physician who attended him was most learned, the court physician from an allied kingdom in the mountains, but even he could not cure the mysterious illness that had come upon the prince of a sudden. All through the feast, the prince lay upon his litter, eating no bite of food and tasting no wine. Duncan saw how the prince tried to smile and be of good cheer, and again Duncan admired his courage. All through the dinner, the king's brother sat at his nephew's side and encouraged him to eat.

When the last bones had been thrown to the dogs, the king summoned Duncan. "Now you have been at court one day. What have you learned?"

Duncan said, "I have learned that the king's brother expects to sit upon the throne."

At that, the court grew still and silent. The king's brother glared at Duncan. The king's face reddened. "It is treason to speak such words of the royal family!"

The prince struggled to sit up and said, "Please, father…"

But the king did not wait to hear what the prince had to say. "This boy shall yet be our guest at court," the king said, "but I have different quarters in mind for him now." And Duncan was thrown into the dungeon.

VI

Duncan sat in the driest corner of the cell, which was not very dry at all. He shivered and wished he had his former clothes, for though tattered, they had been warm.

As Duncan despaired, his cat stepped through the iron bars of the door. In its jaws, the cat carried a mouse so fat that it could only have come from the royal kitchen. The cat lifted each paw in turn to shake off the damp, then set to eating dinner.

Duncan rested his forehead on his knees and said, "Oh, my little cat, what am I to do? I dreamed of seeing the palace, but not this part of it!"

A voice answered, "There is ever so much to smell."

Duncan raised his head. Who else but the cat could have spoken? Duncan said, "Little cat, little cat, what did you say?" But the cat did not look up. It crunched mouse bones as if it knew very well that Duncan had heard. When the cat had eaten the very last morsel, it sniffed the moist floor where the meal had been, then sniffed the air.

"What is there to smell but the damp and rot?" Duncan asked. But he breathed in through his nose. He smelled the wet stones of his cell, and also the rusty smell of the iron door and its lock. He smelled mold and mildew and the stench of royal sewers. When his cat drew near, he smelled a trace of mouse flesh on its breath. None of these smells pleased Duncan, but it was true even here in the dungeon: There was ever so much to smell.

VII

After Duncan had been three days in the dungeon, the king sent for him to see what he had to say for himself now. Duncan bowed before the throne, bowed again to the prince on his litter, and bowed even to the king's brother. "I meant no treason," he said. "Your Highness asked me a question, and I spoke only the truth."

The king frowned, but the prince said, "Is it not as I said? This boy is a simple fisherman, and when he speaks it is with the simple truth. There is no treason in his words if my uncle does in truth expect to be king, and who at court does not expect that? If I am not made well, father, it seems that I shall die before you."

At these words, the king grew pale. The uncle assured the prince that he would surely recover and one day take the throne. But the prince's gaze never left Duncan. "Come forward," he said. When Duncan drew near, he could smell the powders that perfumed the prince's clothes, as well as the mustiness of the prince's sickbed. "We have treated you ill," said the prince, "for you have given us only kindness and honesty. If my father will grant permission, I restore your presence at court."

The king's jaw was set, but he nodded.

Duncan bowed again, and as he did so, he smelled the faintest hint of something both fishy and bitter on the prince's breath.

"My Prince," Duncan said, "you are being poisoned."

The king's brother laughed, perhaps a bit nervously. "The prince is served by a learned physician who knows more than a fisherman knows of poisons."

"Your Highness," said Duncan. "I do not doubt that the physician is a learned man, but is he not a man of the mountains? The poison given to the prince is a poison of the sea."

Now the king's brother grew pale. The king gave Duncan leave to make a search, and two guards to go with him, and they went straightaway to the royal kitchens. Duncan wasted no time as lifted lids from jars and sniffed at shelves as a cat might do. The cook protested this intrusion, but her protest changed to weeping when Duncan's nose led him to a scrap of burlap inside a flour bin. Wrapped in the burlap was a black bit of dried fish liver, roughened on all sides as it had been nicked and shaved away a little at a time.

When she was brought before the king, the cook confessed and accused the king's brother, who had of a sudden made himself scarce. The palace was searched, and then the forest around the palace, and then the entire kingdom. But the king's red-bearded brother was nowhere to be found, and it was supposed that he had chosen exile before justice. It is sad to say that the cook alone was given the reward that she and the king's brother had earned together. If you know anything of kings you can well imagine how she suffered, and if you know nothing of kings then it is a mercy not to tell you.

VIII

The prince, once he was no longer given poison, recovered his usual vigor. Duncan, for his service to the court, was made a courtier for life and given a little room—much drier and pleasanter than his first one. His cat shared the room and also had the freedom of the palace.

In time, the king died and the prince became the new king. Duncan was the man whose eyes and ears and even nose the new king trusted most, and he trusted Duncan to tell the truth when asked for it.

With the passing of years, the cat grew old and fat, but it never spoke again...unless it was the cat who Duncan heard one night long after a royal feast. Duncan had fallen asleep at the table. No one woke him when the king and courtiers all left the great hall. The dishes and table scraps were left for morning, and the lights were put out. Duncan woke in darkness. He heard what might have been the sound of cat feet alighting on the table. He heard a familiar little voice that might have been a cat's voice. It said: "There is ever so much to taste!"

"Little cat, little cat," said Duncan. "What did you say?"

But there came no reply other than the crunch of a chicken bone.

Introduction to "In the Matter of the Ukdena"

"In the Matter of the Ukdena" was reprinted in *The Year's Best Fantasy & Horror* as a fantasy story, but in spite of the magical beings that play a pivotal role, I think this story is closer to science fiction. It is alternate history. What if the natives of North America had been given a little more time to develop resistence to European diseases and European aggression? What if, rather than a conquest, there had been more of a blending of cultures on this continent?

In the Matter of the Ukdena

Spiral Mind turns in on itself,
thinking about the story
of its own nature.

There are many versions
of the story Spiral Mind
is thinking.

Here is one.

Of course, the story can't begin
until there is a universe to contain it.
Spiral Mind says,
Manifestation began in formlessness.
That's how the story gets started,
with the making of a place,
a sky above.
This story begins in the time
when everyone lived in the sky.
Spiral Mind names this time
The First World of the original era.

Clearly, geography is destiny, and a rivalry between the Superpowers was clear as far back as 1850 when Alexis de Tocqueville wrote that he foresaw the development of two principal powers in the world: Imperial Russia, and the United Nations of Turtle Island. "Both countries control an abundance of natural resources," de Tocqueville wrote after his visit to North America, "but the exploitation of those resources is a matter of command in Russia. In the United Nations, the use of resources is controlled by democratic forces and elaborate religious restraints."

> It was crowded in the sky.
> The human beings, the spirits, the gods,
> the two-leggeds and the four-leggeds,
> people with wings like Eagle
> and the crawling people like Ant
> and the digging people like Badger
> and swimmers like Box Turtle,
> the grasses and trees,
> even the stone people
> all crowded in
> together.

Aluminum extraction relies on a process devised simultaneously by Charles Martin Hall in the U.N.T.I and Paul Héroult in France. In this process, alumina (aluminum oxide) is dissolved in molten cryolite and electric current is passed through the solution. At the cathode, metallic aluminum is liberated while oxygen collects at the anode. For the sake of clarity, this chapter will concentrate entirely on the technical aspects of the process. Spiritual considerations on the extraction of metals from the earth, our mother, will be covered in the chapter to follow.

> Water Beetle came down to look around
> before there was any land.
> He dove under the waves
> and surfaced with mud
> in his jaws.
> The Creator Spirits
> rolled the mud in their hands.
> It grew. It became islands.
> Everyone came down.
>
> The human beings came down.
> They were red and brown and black,
> they were white and yellow,
> and they started in their own places,
> but did not stay there.
> They spread themselves out
> as far as possible.
> Wherever they were,
> they walked until oceans stopped them.
>
> Even back when this
> world was new,
> that's how
> they were.
> That's how

> human beings
> have always been.

Aroism (from Spanish, aro, hoop), European term for the plurality of religious beliefs and practices to which the vast majority of North Americans adhere. Arising initially as a synthesis of indigenous beliefs and the religions brought to the Americas by Europeans, Aroism has developed in syncretism with the religious and cultural evolution of the hemisphere. Aroist belief is generally characterized by sacralization of all phenomena, but special emphasis is given to particular sacred locales and to Mother Earth in general. Similar in some aspects to **Animism**, Aroism calls upon believers to communicate with the natural world as they interact with it so that their actions may be in harmony with the natural order. As Western technological practices such as mining and deep-furrow agriculture were introduced, Aroist beliefs evolved to allow for resource exploitation consistent with sacred regard for the earth. Most Aroists adhere to traditions of **Vision Quest**, **Ritual Purification** and, for women, **Moon Lodge**.

> The white tribes
> on their part of the world
> were as varied as any people,
> but there were some things
> most of them believed.

"I'll tell you," said the keynote speaker at the Conference for

Spiritual History, "what the white nations of Europe believed. They believed that children were little bags of sin to be redeemed by beatings. They believed in the authority of a God King, in the authority of human kings, in the authority of men over women."

> The white tribes believed in a universe divided
> between good and evil,
> in a world that was theirs to master
> if they could only destroy enough
> of the evil.
>
> Don't get the idea
> that these people were creatures of darkness.
> Any human being can carry light.

```
From:V. Adm. David Many Bears
Fleet Operations
To:Capt. Henry Jefferson
U.N.S. Nimitz
```

Hank, this is going to come down to you through channels, but before it does I wanted you to have some advance notice of the new policy regarding Navy fighter jets for use in vision quests. NAFCOM acknowledges the right of pilots and their RIOs to use any means at their disposal to seek a vision, but loss of an Ukdena in the Sixth Fleet's carrier group has lead us to formulate what you might call Rules of Engagement with the Great Mystery.

The F-4 Ukdena is rated at a service ceiling of 43,000 at power, but the crew of the Sixth Fleet mishap had throttled up hard and gone to 56,000.

Hank, you and I both know how imminent the Great Mystery must be at ten miles above the earth, but we also know that this was a thousand feet above the fleet-configured F-4's maximum rating. A pilot in combat won't make a mistake like that, but a pilot who's flying into the sun can get a little lost up there.

From now on, each crew is allowed one official quest flight per deployment, and they aren't to climb above the military-power service ceiling. I know that there will be some grumbling about this, and I know that there will be covert questing beyond what we're officially sanctioning, but this will at least make it clear that the pain of the sundance is meant for the body, not the airframe of a fighter plane.

> The red tribes
> on this Turtle Island
> were as varied as any people,
> but most of them tried to discover
> right relation to one another
> and to the earth.
> The red tribes believed in
> the spiral,
> the circle,

and everything
was alive.

Don't get the idea
that these people were flames of enlightenment.
Any human being drags a shadow.

Sequoyah, 1766-1843, Tsalagi. First president of the U.N.T.I., commander in chief of the Continental Army in the War of Union, called the Father of His Country. He created a syllabary for the Tsalagi language, based on the characters he saw for English and Spanish writing, providing the model for the **Universal Writing System**.

New Etowah, capital of the U.N.T.I., co-extensive with the District of Sequoyah.

Andrew Jackson, 1767-1832. White separatist leader. After his defeat by units of the Creek Nation in the battle of Horseshoe Bend, Jackson escaped and continued to lead Europeans opposed to national assimilation. Convinced that his vision of a European-dominated culture could take root in the west, he led his erstwhile followers on an ill-fated forced march. See **Trail of Tears**.

In those times
before the white people came to Turtle Island
the Tsalagi, the Principal People,
lived in the mountains
that were at the middle of the earth.

They wanted

peace at the center of all things.
At the center of all things,
harmony.

Late in the last year of the eleventh heaven,
seven generations before the first hell
of the Fifth World,
the days and nights came into
balance
and the cornstalks grew heavy
with grain,
so the Principal People began the Green Corn Ceremony
that would preserve harmony for all beings.

In the council houses of many villages,
the Tsalagi danced and made offerings
to the sacred fire.
In the rivers
they bathed seven times
for purity
and held rituals
to turn aside any anger
left over
from the year they were about to finish.

"What can we reliably say about Spiritual History in pre-literate times?" said the keynote speaker. "To a large extent, we must rely upon the oral tradition. Spiral-thought does not record events with the same emphasis that Arrow-thought does, of course, so we do not remember the details of the political discussions, the names, dates, and exact locations of the debates. But we know, generally, what was decided in the matter of the Ukdena, and we know that it was probably decided in Green Corn time. To this day, that remains the best time for establishing national policy."

Before he went to sleep after the fifth day of deliberations, Walks the River made an offering of cedar smoke to the four directions, to heaven, and to earth. The open eaves of his wife's summer house let the smoke drift away, but the scent remained behind to clear his thoughts and purify his dreams. Though the fire was low, he could see that his wife was watching him with the same expression she had worn during the council, a mixture of discomfort and expectation. There might have been impatience in that gaze, too, except that she was an old Tsalagi woman, a Bird clan woman. She knew how to master herself. She knew how to turn impatience aside, for the sake of harmony.

Silently, Walks the River asked for dreams that would help him carry light. Then, with limbs stiffened by the chill air, he lay down beside his wife.

"It has been five days," she said. She said it gently, sleepily, as if in answer to a question.

"Yes," he said, keeping his voice level. "I have counted them, too."

If she divorced him, he could always go live in his sister's house. It pained him to think such a thought, and he doubted that his wife would turn him out, but who would blame her if she did? What was worse than for a man to seem stubborn and argumentative at the holiest time of the year?

He waited, but she said nothing more. Soon she was breathing the breath of sleep. He heard one of his daughters whisper to her husband in a far corner of the lodge, and an ember popped in the fire.

Give me a dream, he prayed again. Let me see them in my dream.

And then he let the night sounds carry him, the sounds of dark water in the river and wind moving through the trees. Those sounds were still in his ears when he crossed into the dream side of the world and found himself standing on an unfamiliar mountain's grassy bald. Around him were other mountains, covered with fir and spruce. He raised his hands into the dream sky, asking for bountiful life, a prayer for his arrival.

Light dazzled him. Something huge was there in front of him, making the air near him hiss with its passing, and then it was far away. It moved partly in the air and partly along a mountain ridge, making the trees sway. He wanted to see it clearly, but it was not a thing the eyes could easily hold.

"Ukdena," he said.

"Ukdena," he prayed.

The presence swirled high into the air. It was not one being, but a group. They twisted and twined together, parted, and rushed together again. They moved from one side of the sky to the other. Walks the River squinted.

Their scales flashed like facets of crystal. Their bodies were long, sinuous, humping and curving as though even in the sky they had to follow the lines of the mountain ridges below. Once, he thought he caught a glimpse of transparent wings, and for a moment there seemed to be an eye that gazed at him, cold and brilliant.

For a long time he dreamed this dream. Claws. They had terrible claws, glittering like ice, opening and closing on the wind.

"What do you want us to do?" he asked them. "What do you want?" They danced their dance and glittered and burst into flames that didn't harm them. They roared like a forest on fire.

When he awoke, he was careful not to move. That way he could hold the memory a little longer. Then at last he sat up, filled with sadness because he was more firmly trapped than ever. This would be the sixth day of council, but the dream had only strengthened his resolve. He rose quietly and dressed, slipping out of his wife's house before she and her daughters could wake up to repeatedly ask no one in particular when the council would be over.

He went to watch the river. There was, as far as he could see, no right way to act. If he continued to argue, he brought discord into the council house. If he withdrew, he betrayed both the Ukdena and his own heart.

Of course, if he no longer had the support of his clan, then the matter would come to an end. What mattered was not his opinion, but the consensus of the village's Wild Potato clan. Perhaps his people could no longer bear the shame of contentious words spoken in their name.

He went to his sister's lodge to eat breakfast, rather than returning to the Bird clan household of his wife, and then he began to test the opinions of his people. His sister and her grown daughters supported him, but there was certainly more to the clan than his closest family.

He greeted White Clay Woman by the doorway of her house, working in the morning light.

"Good day, Beloved Man," she answered as she sewed feathers onto her new cape. At her feet were songbirds, not yet plucked of feathers for the cape's fringe. "Has your heart changed in the night?"

"No," he told her. "But I am afraid that it is time for us to withdraw."

"Is that what your dreams told you?"

"No," he admitted.

"Then speak your heart," White Clay Woman told him. "I am with you."

Eye Covered, who was guarding her corn from crows, said she had no opinion and just kept asking Walks the River to bring her water to drink, or to watch the field while she fetched it herself. He brought her water, and then she told him he should follow his heart in the matter of the Ukdena. He asked her again, just to be sure she was not merely being polite. "What do your dreams say?" she said.

With the men who were catching fish, it was the same. Walks the River watched them dam the fishing stream, and then a man named Runner threw ground horse chestnuts into the shadowed pools of still water where the fish hid themselves.

"The other clans are in agreement," Walks the River said. "We are the only holdouts. I begin to feel that we are not behaving well."

The men waiting for the fish asked him if his dreams had changed, and he said again that they had not.

"Every night," one young man said as he stirred the water, "I pray for all my relations. The Ukdena, too, are my relations."

The first of the paralyzed fish floated to the surface. The young men began to choose the ones they wanted and loaded them into baskets. Soon they had all they wanted.

Walks the River looked through the foliage, seeing light from the ridge line glint between the trees. He had never seen the Ukdena in the waking world, but the priests saw them all the time. "The Ukdena are our relations," he agreed. "But I will not shame the clan."

"Do not stand aside until you are almost moved to anger," advised Runner. "We are all of one heart. The Ukdena should be maintained." He opened the dam, and fresh water rushed into the pools. The remaining fish soon recovered and dove back down into the deeper water.

"People think impatient thoughts," Walks the River said.

"As long as you do not become angry," another man said, "there is only a little shame. We can bear it."

So it was that on the sixth day of the council Walks the River sat in the circle of seven Beloved Men with his resolve unbent. Behind him sat the people of the Wild Potato clan, and he could feel their support still flowing to him, even in the face of unified opposition.

In the center of the circle of Beloved Men stood the principal priest, the second priest, and Red Fox, who was the secular officer.

As if he had not already put the question to them a score of times already, the principal priest said, "In the matter of the Ukdena and a third priest, how are we resolved?"

"As we have heard," said Woods Burning, the Beloved Man of the Deer clan, "The Ukdena are growing fewer." He looked at Walks the River and the Wild Potato clan behind him. "We acknowledge that this is true. And fewer priests train to control the energies of the Ukdena. That also is true. But is this bad? The Ukdena are dangerous, so it is a good thing that there are fewer of them. And since there are fewer of them, we need fewer priests to control them. Therefore, in the matter of a third priest for the village who would learn the ways of the Ukdena and carry the objects that control them, let it be resolved that we shall not support such a priest. We have two priests already. That is enough."

The other Beloved Men spoke in turn. For the Wolf clan and the Long Hair clan, they spoke. For the Paint clan and the Blue clan and the Bird clan. All agreed that the village would not support a third priest, that maintaining the Ukdena was too costly a task for a village of their size to take on.

"I have considered," said Walks the River, "and I have dreamed." For a moment, he could feel the hope that filled the lodge, the expectation that he was going to throw in with the rest and make the opinion unanimous and harmonious at last.

"The Ukdena are growing fewer because there are fewer priests to master them and hold them to the earth. Yes, the Ukdena are dangerous, but under the control of the Principal People they are dangerous only to our enemies."

The disappointment filled the room like bad air.

"All right," said the second priest. His job was to manage the discussion, and he was allowed no opinion of his own. "Let us consider again the nature of the Ukdena."

"We all know their nature," said Holds the Corn Up, Beloved Man of the Long Hair clan. "They are anger and fear. That is their energy."

"They are the unmastered anger and fear of all the world's people," said Walks the River. "And why does this energy come here, to the Principal People, if not to be guided by us? Why are we together, Tsalagi and Ukdena, in the same place, the middle of the world, if not so that the Principal People might direct those energies safely? We must hold in trust all the powers that attach to us."

"I have had a dream," said the Paint clan's Beloved Man. "In my dream, I saw the Great Bear dancing, stomping."

Everyone had that dream sooner or later, and everyone understood what it meant. The Great Bear was stamping out fear and ignorance from the world.

"I think," the man continued, "that the Ukdena are the very thing that the Great Bear is trying to drive out of the earth with his dancing."

"No power is all good or all bad," said Walks the River. "In my dreams, I have seen the Ukdena, and they are beautiful."

The secondary priest said, "The man who has not mastered himself looks at the Ukdena and sees demons. But the man who knows his heart and masters clear thought will see angels instead. The Ukdena are the same Ukdena." This was not opinion, but simply a review of the facts.

"It's just a question of one priest," Red Fox reminded everyone.

"Ours is the Very Middle village," said Walks the River, "in the middle of the world. We are at the center of many circles. Already, the science that communicates with the Ukdena and guides them for us is in decline. Our decision may travel from the center like a stone in still water. If we will not maintain the Ukdena, how do we know anyone will? I think that if we make the wrong decision, the Principal People will forget how to master the Ukdena. I can imagine a time when the Ukdena pass out of this world with hardly any notice by our people. What if we call to them and they are no longer here to answer us?"

"Why should we call to them?" said Woods Burning. "Why should we bring down fear and anger to the earth? When is fear good? When is anger good?"

"A man without fear cannot be brave," said Walks the River. "As for anger, it is needed for passion. For justice."

"For justice, we have the law," said Woods Burning. "If the Shaawanwaaki raid our village and kill five people, then we will kill five Shaawanwaaki. If a Blue clan man murders someone in the Long Hair clan, then the killer or someone else in his clan must die. The law maintains harmony. Nothing else is needed."

"Walks the River imagines a time without Ukdena," said the Paint clan's Beloved Man. "I imagine instead a time of abundant Ukdena. If there are too many of these beings held here by our medicine, then no one will be able to contain them. They will range farther and farther from the middle of the world. Other people do not train themselves as we do. Who knows what the wandering Ukdena might do in the lands of people who do not see as clearly as we must see?"

"Neither thing has happened," said Red Fox. "We have always held the Ukdena here in harmony."

"The Ukdena grow fewer," said Walks the River. "That is certain. Who knows what turn the future will take?"

"Is the future singular," said the Beloved Man of the Blue clan, "or is it multiple? Is there one future, or many?"

"The future shall unfold according to prophecy," said Holds the Corn.

"Yes," agreed Woods Burning, "but many paths possible to the same point in prophecy."

The principal priest said, "In the matter of the Ukdena and a third priest, how are we resolved?"

Again, the Beloved Men of the majority clans spoke their positions. Nothing had changed. Walks the River looked at his bony hands and bit his lip. What else was there to do? All of his arguments had been repeated many times. He had not moved any of the others, and he had not himself been moved to join them.

Politeness dictated that he should withdraw now. He and all of his clan should leave the council house so that the decision could be made unanimously in their absence. That was not what he wanted to do, but how could he stay and still believe himself a reasonable man?

Clearly he must withdraw.

But he waited. He thought of what the Blue clan speaker had just said. Was there one future, or many? Perhaps he was now at the place where the futures divided like channels of a river moving around a great stone. He was the great stone. If he leaned one way, this channel would be the greater. Lean the other way, and the other channel would determine how prophecy would be fulfilled.

And what prophecy was it that was flowing around him? What futures might depend on him?

The Ukdena were beautiful. The Ukdena were terrible. Harmony was beautiful and holy, but was it better preserved by defending the Ukdena or by letting the matter drop?

Continue or withdraw? Each choice seemed both right and wrong.

"We will not be moved," he said for his clan.

People in the Council House shifted around, as if feeling for the first time the stiffness of sitting for many days. The Beloved Men of the other clans looked over their shoulders to read the eyes of their people.

After a time the speaker for the Wolf clan turned to face the priests and the sacred fire. "It is the sixth day," he said. "For six days, the Wild Potato clan has not moved. Nothing moves them, and they do not turn aside. Walks the River is a thoughtful and well-mannered man. He bears a lot and does not anger. This begins to change our hearts. We say there shall be a third priest, and he shall learn to master the Ukdena."

That was how the tide turned, but politics flow slowly. It was not until late in the next day that the Blue clan and Deer clan supported the training of a new priest.

"Think of the Great Bear, stamping on the ground," the Paint clan's Beloved Man argued, though the flow had clearly shifted against him. "Fear and ignorance, that's what he tramples down. Let the Ukdena decline. We don't need them. We do not need a third priest."

But it was after this speech that Holds the Corn had brought the Long Hair clan to the other side, in favor of maintaining an additional priest. Woods Burning felt his own clan shift beneath him, and whatever his own feelings, he had to speak for his people. "Let there be a third priest," he said.

The Paint clan held their ground until the end of that seventh day. Their Beloved Man argued about the risks of crowding the skies with Ukdena, but too many Ukdena seemed a less plausible future than a future where the last Ukdena had vibrated itself out of this world. Everyone had already agreed that the Ukdena were in decline.

In the end, the Paint clan could not agree with the majority, but they left the Council House and let the village make a unanimous decision in their absence.

"In the matter of the Ukdena and a third priest," said the principal priest, "how are we resolved?"

"That there shall be a third priest so that we may remember how to hold the Ukdena to the earth," said Red Fox. "That is the decision of all the people."

If any Tsalagi were angry over the outcome, they turned their anger aside and it did not show. The village held the form of harmony, and the sacred fire was extinguished. The last year of the eleventh heaven was over. The priests kindled a new fire in the Council House, and women carried embers from it into each home. The people carried their new clothes to the river, and then they bathed, letting the current carry away their old clothing and the old year with it. When they stepped ashore to dress in new garments, they were themselves renewed. It was the twelfth heaven, seven generations before the first hell of the Fifth World.

Walks the River did not dream of the Ukdena again, and in the year that followed, he died in his sleep. Many Beloved Men died in that year, but they had lived long enough, at least, to see the twelfth heaven.

The keynote speaker said, "The extent to which Ukdena-mind became prevalent on Turtle Island is evident in the report of Bernal Díaz del Castillo, a sailor in Hernando de Soto's 'discovery' voyage, who wrote that the crew saw 'dragons' in the air above Cuba. Some researchers have even speculated that a forgotten earlier explorer, a Genoan called Cristobal Colón, made landfall in the Americas fifty years ahead of de Soto. Ukdena-mind, and the fear and suspicion it often generates if unchecked, could explain what happened to this Colón. As was the case for de Soto, it's almost certain that the Caribs would have welcomed him with arrows. De Soto himself narrowly escaped the destruction of his fleet on his first voyage. But this earlier landfall and contact would explain the arrival of smallpox on the continent two generations before the first significant wave of European invaders. Our history might have been very different if, without two generations of previous exposure to the disease, the native peoples had been forced to contend simultaneously with aggressive invaders and a virulent disease to which they had no time to build immune resistance."

>
> Almost with the speed of Ukdena,
> the sickness crossed the water between islands,
> entered the low country of the Apalachee
> rose into the mountains of the Tsalagi.
> From the Tsalagi homeland
> in the middle of the world
> the disease spread
> in all directions.
>
> People died.
> Young and old
> they died.
> Potawatomi and Kansa
> Kiowa and Paiute
> Shuswap and Shoshoni
> Chiricahua and Azteca
> they died.
> That was during the first hell
> of the Fifth World.
> So many people died
> That Turtle Island seemed empty.
>
> But the ones who survived,
> they were the strong human beings,
> the ones the sickness couldn't easily kill,
> and their children were also strong.
> The disease kept coming back,
> but every time

> the people were stronger
> and the disease could not kill
> so easily.

"As opposed to Africa," the speaker said, "development of cultural exchange took a very different turn in the 'new' world, thanks to this pattern of successful resistance. Rather than cultural conquest or even cultural hegemony, the North American continent experienced something like a cultural marriage and an exchange between equals. Some of what was traded was tangible, as in the exchange of maize for wheat. Other trades were more subtle. Europeans learned how to hold the Forms of Peace. The Turtle Island Nations were introduced to the concept of the Nation State. It was this more subtle trade that effected the greatest change in both cultures. Europeans gradually stopped thinking of themselves as clever for accepting more gifts than they gave. There may be an objective sense in which it's true that, as the Ukdena priests say, this continent is built on the energies of Ukdena-mind."

> The river of prophecy
> is one river.
>
> The current weaves and divides,
> but water always flows
> downhill.
>
> Perhaps there is more
> than one reality.
>
> Spiral mind is wide enough
> to contain another universe.

❖ ❖ ❖

"I can sum up Indian history in the United States of America in very few words," said the keynoter at a conference in Washington, D.C., the nation's capitol. "The Trail of Tears. Sand Creek. Wounded Knee. We can imagine how things might have been different, but we're confronted nonetheless with how things were, and are. But I also want you to consider this. Where did the people of this continent go? They did not all die in the American genocide, though nine-tenths of them did. Their descendants are not all living on reservations, though many are, trapped there as a matter of public policy. But where are the rest?

"Let me frame it in another way. No conqueror is left unaffected by the conquest. Consider that in the United States of America today we have people who look like Europeans who will chain themselves to a tree and risk death for the sake of an owl. I'm talking about a process that goes both ways, of course. There are also people who look like Indians who will lease their tribal lands to strip miners. Who, then, is more Indian? Who is more white? Where are the Indians now? Where are the Europeans?"

Some would say that the effect of all those secret grandmothers, Indian women giving birth to and raising children in families that were designated "black" or "white," has been the **Indianization** of the majority culture. In this view, a lot of secret wisdom was passed down along with that secret blood. Proponents of this notion point out that the very attributes considered by the Europeans to be marks of savagery sound like a portrait of the still-evolving American culture: permissive child rearing; the habit of bathing more often than "necessary"; suspicion of "authority"; passionate pride; acceptance and empowerment of women and of more than one sexual norm; fluid class distinctions, or no such distinctions at all.

On Turtle Island
Arrow Mind and Spiral Mind
twine and twist
together.

It is one mind now.

In any version of the story,
it is one mind.

Introduction to
"Twas the Night Before Global Economic Integration"

The Lexus and the Olive Tree by Thomas L. Friedman is a very thoughtful look at the effects of globalization. Who knew that it would inspire a story about Santa Claus?

Twas the Night Before Global Economic Integration

Niles, the lead elf in the wooden toy division and union president, couldn't believe what he'd just heard. "You're canning us? And on the day before Christmas?"

Santa Claus sighed sympathetically. "I had hoped to do this through attrition, Niles, but it's been six hundred years since an elf retired. And things had to change."

"Had to change? What are you talking about?"

"I'm talking about globalization," Santa said. "It's a fast world these days. If you can't adapt, you go under. That's how it is." He patted Niles on the head. "I'm sorry. We've been operating at a loss."

The elf batted Santa's hand away. "Are you crazy? We've *always* operated at a loss."

"Yes, on finite resources. It couldn't go on forever."

"Without elves, who's going to make the toys? Who's going to take care of the reindeer?"

"The reindeer are already gone, air-freighted to a retirement pasture in Lapland. As for making the toys, the same subcontractor who is streamlining the transportation division will be handling that."

"Subcontractor?"

Santa pointed out the window toward the warehouse. Niles

put his hands on the sill and looked out. Standing next to the warehouse was a building on stilts. Stilts that shivered in the cold. No, they weren't stilts at all. They were chicken legs. It was a little house standing on enormous chicken legs.

Niles said, "Gross. What is that? It wasn't there when I came in."

"It moves with absolute silence, even quieter than the sleigh. And as for capacity, well, you can see that I'll need to make far fewer trips."

"What *is* it?"

"The hut of Baba Yaga, the Russian witch."

"A witch? You're replacing us with a witch?"

"I know it seems an unlikely alliance," Santa said as he sat down behind his desk, "but she backed up her proposal with some attractive numbers. If you take a look at this spreadsheet…"

"You know where you can put that spreadsheet," Niles said. "You may have timed this so we can't go on strike, but that doesn't mean that we'll take this lying down!"

Santa pressed a button on his desk. "I'm sorry you feel that way." The office door opened and two security guards came inside. "These gentlemen will escort you off the grounds."

Santa watched the elf go. Other pairs of guards were escorting other elves. Santa shook his head and sighed. Was he making a mistake? He looked at the spreadsheet numbers. No, this was how it had to be. It was a fast world now. If you couldn't adapt, you'd go under. He sat behind his desk thinking, then got up to warm his hands by the fire. Then he paced.

Perhaps he'd feel better if he went to Baba Yaga's hut for some tea. He needed to discuss the night's work schedule with her, anyway. He stepped outside, closed the door behind him, and found, when he looked up, that the hut of Baba Yaga was gone. And it wasn't just somewhere else on the grounds. He checked the elves' dormitory courtyard. He looked behind the empty reindeer stables. The hut had vanished.

Worse, the toy warehouse was empty. There was no positive interpretation that Santa could give this situation. Baba Yaga wasn't just taking a load of toys for a test run. It would have taken multiple trips to empty the warehouse. Santa had been ripped off. Without reindeer, he had no way to pursue the witch.

"I'm ruined," he groaned. He put his head in his hands. He wept. And he heard…sleigh bells.

Santa looked up. A troika drawn by three black horses approached. A man in a blue coat trimmed with fur held the reins. There was a beautiful young woman on the seat beside him, and a man in a black business suit next to her. "Ho, ho, ho!" the driver said. His beard was as long and white as Santa's. A bag of presents lay in the back of the troika. "Having little bit of trouble?" the driver said. He gave the reins to the girl and stepped down. "You need help, da?"

"Who are you?"

"You don't know? Russian counterpart, Ded Moroz." He held out a bony hand.

"Dead Morose?"

"Make fun all you like, but you need me. You made contract with witch Baba Yaga. Big mistake. Snegurochka and I always have trouble with her at Christmas. She is big present thief, that Baba Yaga."

"Snego…"

"Snegurochka. My lovely…granddaughter." Ded Moroz indicated the girl. She smiled at Santa with a smile that said many things. One thing that it said was that she was not Ded Moroz's granddaughter. "We knew if you accepted Baba Yaga's offer it would create trouble for you."

"You knew this was going to happen? Why didn't you warn me?"

"In business you do your own due diligence, da? We have experience dealing with witch. You want help?"

"You can get the presents back? We can save Christmas? Then of course I want your help!"

"Good. This man is attorney. He has papers you must sign."

"Papers?"

"Merger agreement. Santa Claus becomes wholly owned subsidiary of Grandfather Frost." Ded Moroz pointed to himself.

"Wholly owned... You're buying me out?"

"Don't worry. Your operations change little in first few years. Eventually, you retire with nice pension to dacha on Black Sea." He nodded at the attorney, who got down from the troika and opened his briefcase.

"But, but I'm Santa Claus! I can't retire! Who will bring presents to all the good children?"

"Times change," said Ded Moroz. "Capitalist system rewards best service. I bring presents on Orthodox Christmas *and* New Years Day. Kids get presents from me just for being kids, not for being nice. Also, they don't have to write me letters, so everything is easier for them. Grownups like me, too. Ded Moroz is more fun at parties. I like vodka. I bring Snegurochka along." He winked. "She is fun at parties, too."

"But," Santa said, "I'm the tradition in many parts of the world."

"Global marketplace now. You move fast, or you fall behind. You sign now."

The attorney gave Santa a sheaf of papers and a pen. "Sign here and here and initial every page," he said.

Santa took the pen in a trembling hand. He hesitated. Then he signed.

"Ho, ho, ho," said Ded Moroz as he opened a bottle. He filled a glass for everyone.

Snegurochka smiled a pretty smile. "*S Rozhdestvom Hristovym!*" she said, lifting her drink.

"Yeah," said Santa. He slugged the vodka down. "Merry Christmas to us all."

Introduction to "Okra, Sorghum, Yam"

Just as "Half of the Empire" relies of the traditional structure of a fairy tale, "Okra, Sorghum, Yam" requires readers who are familiar with the formula of the three siblings: The first son tries and fails. The second son tries and fails. The third son, who no one has any hope for, tries…and succeeds. When we know a story so well, perhaps it's unnecessary for the teller to tell it all.

Okra, Sorghum, Yam

So the following summer when the second princess came to Old Kwaku's hut, he said, "What do *you* want?"

"My father said that I must learn wisdom from you."

"And is that what you want?"

"I wouldn't mind being wise, but when my sister returned from here last summer her hands were rough and red. She said she hadn't learned anything at all. What if I go home like that? What man will marry a princess who has a farmer's hands?"

"And if you must work to become wise?"

"I hope that you'll have better luck than with my sister, however you do it. Make me wise, and my father will be pleased. The he will marry me to a prince rich in goats and cattle. I'll dress in fine clothes and have twice as many servants as I have now."

"So it's wisdom you want?"

"Do I look like a girl who wastes her time? Yes, I want wisdom! Stop asking the same question and get on with it!"

So Old Kwaku, he told her what he had told her sister, that she must work with him in the fields all summer and through the harvest if she wanted to learn wisdom. She didn't like that idea one bit, but she couldn't go back to her father and say that she hadn't tried.

In his vegetable garden, Old Kwaku planted collard and okra and cowpeas. He showed the second princess how to cut the weeds down with a sharpened stick.

"I don't think I'm learning any wisdom," she said. "And look at my hands! Imagine what they'll look like at the end of the summer!"

"Here is part of wisdom," Old Kwaku said, and he began to rearrange some okra pods while they were still on their mother plants. He pulled one and nudged another and coaxed a third. He moved this one and that one together and tied the pods together in the shape of a little green person.

"That doesn't look like wisdom to me," the princess said. "Oh, I'm going to go home and die in my father's house, an old maid!"

Elsewhere, Old Kwaku had planted sorghum. He gave the princess a strip of cloth to wave to scare the birds away from the ripening grain.

"This cloth is rough," she said. "When I am married to a rich man, I hope that nothing this coarse will ever touch my skin! I will lie in the shade while other people work, when wisdom has made me into an excellent bride."

"Here is part of wisdom," Old Kwaku told her, and he began to bend this plant gently toward that one and to tie some of the seed heads together. Torso, arms, legs, and head. He tied the sorghum into the shape of a person.

"That doesn't look like wisdom to me," she said. "I hope I start seeing soon what this has to do with wisdom."

In another place, Old Kwaku grew yams. He showed the princess how to clear the weeds and grasses away from the vines, and then he had her dig very carefully to expose some of the tubers without damaging them. He had her pour water from an earthen jar to wash the yams while they were still in the ground.

She stood up and flung mud from her fingers. "Digging in the dirt is no way to learn wisdom! You're taking advantage of me! Show me some wisdom right now!"

"Here is part of wisdom," Old Kwaku said. Gently, he moved the yams without pulling them free. He positioned two to be the arms, two to be the legs, one for the trunk and one for the head. Sure enough, he had put yams together in the shape of a person. He gently pushed the soil back over them.

"That doesn't look like wisdom to me," said the princess. "I should break that water jar over your head!" She stomped off to the river to wash her hands.

When it was time, Old Kwaku harvested the crops, all except for the figures made of okra, sorghum, and yams. He made a great big pot of stew, but he did not taste it and he did not let the princess have any, either. "Soon you'll return to your father, with wisdom or without," he told her. "We'll fast tonight. Beginning tomorrow, let us feast for three days and see whether, at the end, you are wise."

The princess didn't want to fast, but Old Kwaku slept by the pot with the ladle in his hand, like a guard with his spear. So the princess went to bed hungry for the first time in her life. When she woke up, she was very hungry indeed. Old Kwaku was already awake. He had set out three bowls on the mat. The princess knelt down before one, but Old Kwaku said, "We must wait for our guest."

Just then, a tiny voice called out, "I am here for now, but I'm afraid I'm not here for long!"

"Come in, come in," said Old Kwaku. "We were expecting you." He pulled aside the mat that covered his door, and in came a little green person made of okra. Old Kwaku filled the bowls and knelt before one.

As the princess reached for her bowl, the little okra person went to the third bowl and peered inside. "What if it's poisoned?"

The princess looked at her stew. Old Kwaku took a taste from his own bowl and said, "It's not poisoned."

"But how do we know," said the okra person, "that you didn't poison only mine? Or hers?"

"You saw me dish them out."

"Ah, but you're sly," said the okra person. "We weren't watching you carefully. And even if *you* are innocent, a witch might have poisoned it all while you slept."

The princess was very hungry, but now she sat looking at her stew without eating it.

"What do you care if you are poisoned in the morning?" asked Old Kwaku, eating some more of his stew. "You are going to die anyway when the sun goes down."

"Why did you have to remind me?" shouted the okra person in a voice so shrill that the princess had to cover her ears. "I don't want to die! Will I suffer? I don't want to be in pain! What is death, anyway? Is it only the beginning of more suffering? Poor me! I am going to a place of torment, I just know it! When will it happen? How high is the sun? How much time is left to me?" The little okra person cried and fretted and cried some more. The princess sat with her hands over her ears all day. Old Kwaku calmly finished his stew, then dumped the untouched servings of the princess and the okra person back into the pot.

When the sun touched the horizon, the okra person ran around in circles, shrieking in terror until it fell down dead. Old Kwaku threw its body into the fire and gave the princess the empty bowls. "Take these to the river and clean them," he said.

"First I want some stew," said the princess.

"No," said Old Kwaku. "Now we must fast until tomorrow. Then we will eat our fill."

The princess took the bowls to the river. She was very, very hungry now. But what if something like this happened again the next day? How could she eat with such a terrible visitor in the hut? What if she starved to death? She brought the clean bowls back and lay down to try to sleep, but she couldn't. She stayed up thinking about herself growing thinner and thinner.

In the morning, Old Kwaku set out three bowls again. The princess was both hungry and tired as she knelt before one. "We must wait for our guest," said Old Kwaku.

From outside, a little voice called, "I'm here for now, and I hope I'll be welcome!"

"Come in, come in," said Old Kwaku. "We were expecting you."

In danced a little brown and white person made of sorghum seeds. Old Kwaku filled three bowls.

As the princess reached for her bowl, the sorghum person said, "I hope this has tender meat in it!"

Meat sounded wonderful to the princess. She smiled at the thought.

"It's a vegetable stew," said Old Kwaku. He tasted his.

"Well I hope it tastes rich. I hope it's as smooth as butter."

The princess held her bowl, thinking of the wonderful taste of butter.

"It tastes as it tastes," said Old Kwaku, eating some more.

The princess was still very, very hungry, but the stew did not seem so appealing, now that she had tender meat and butter on her mind.

The sorghum person said, "Well, I hope we'll have something better tomorrow, something meaty and buttery that we can eat every day for the rest of our lives!"

"But you have only this day to live," said Old Kwaku.

"That's true," said the little sorghum person, beginning to dance around. "Oh, I hope I am going to paradise! I hope I have an easy death, and that in the land of the dead, there is goat meat cooked in milk. Plantains in honey would be tasty. I'd like to have some roasted beef. After I am gone, I hope I won't have to eat ordinary stews. I'll have fish curry with groundnuts!"

The princess forgot that she was holding a bowl of ordinary stew as she watched the little sorghum person dance and listened to it name all the fine things that it would eat in paradise. Old Kwaku finished his stew. When the sun touched the horizon, the sorghum person fell over dead, and Old Kwaku threw it onto the fire where it popped and crackled. He took the princess's bowl from her and dumped the stew back in the pot. He did the same with the third serving and sent the princess to the river to wash the empty bowls.

As she washed the bowls and brought them back, the princess hoped that tomorrow would be better. Hunger gnawed at her when she lay down on her mat. Old Kwaku slept by the pot as before. Perhaps he would fall asleep before she did and she could sneak a taste of stew. But weariness overcame even her hunger, and her eyes closed.

She awoke to the sound of a little voice shouting, "Let me in! I have no time to waste!" She opened her eyes to see that there were already three servings of stew on the mat. A little purple person made of yams entered the hut and stamped across the floor toward the bowls.

"You call this stew?" it said. "I deserve a better feast than this!"

The princess sat up and rubbed the sleep from her eyes. Old Kwaku picked up one of the bowls and began to eat. "It's very good," he said.

"Well, it's not good enough for the likes of me!" insisted the yam person. It tried to overturn one of the bowls, but it wasn't strong enough. "Why are your stupid bowls so heavy?" It kicked the side of the bowl.

"Calm down," said Old Kwaku. "Life is short."

"I know that life is short!" It kicked the bowl again. "I know it!"

The princess reached for one of the bowls, and the yam person said to Old Kwaku, "Aha! I see that you're up to your old tricks, deceiving girls and making them work your fields. Look at her hands!"

The princess looked at her callused hands and stopped reaching for the bowl.

"You got a season's work out of her, and what does she have to show for it? Her body is tired, her belly is empty, and is she wise? She's wise to *you*, maybe! Maybe she's finally catching on, you old fraud!"

The princess closed her hands into fists. She looked at Old Kwaku, who calmly ate his stew. She trembled. "It's true!" she said. "You're nothing but a cheat! I did everything you told me to do, and am I wise?" She seized one of the bowls.

"You are hungry," said Old Kwaku. "Have some stew."

"I'll give you stew!" she shouted. She hurled the bowl to the floor. She picked up the other bowl and broke that one as well. "You promised wisdom and gave me only grief! If I were a man, I would kill you!" On her way out, she tore the mat from the doorway and flung it to the ground.

"Are you going to let her talk to you like that?" the yam person demanded.

Old Kwaku went on eating.

"Those were good bowls!" said the yam person. "How dare she break those bowls!"

When he had eaten his fill, Old Kwaku cleaned up the mess of stew and broken pottery.

"Look! She didn't just rip your mat from the doorway! She tore the mat itself! Your best mat! Why aren't you getting mad? You let her walk all over you! I could just strangle you for being so soft!"

Using some reeds, Old Kwaku mended and rehung the mat. When the sun touched the horizon, the little yam person stamped on the ground, screamed with fury and died. Old Kwaku threw what was left of him onto the fire.

Now the next summer, when the third princess came to visit, it was an altogether different story.

Introduction to
"How the Highland People Came to Be"

Heroic fantasy is usually given a European setting, but warriors, sorcerers and mysterious powers have come in many forms. Trading castles for sun temples changes more than the mere furniture of a story, and for me, that's the reward in setting fantasies in the context of non-European cultures. Of course, the culture I'm describing is an invented one. "How the Highland People Came to Be" is not set in Meso-America any more than *The Lord of the Rings* is set in Europe.

How the Highland People Came to Be

Nictay paused in her leaf gathering. From the jungle shadows, she watched the battlefield. Not long after the Moon warriors had retreated with their captives, women of the Red Crown village had come into the bloodied fields of maize stubble to care for wounded brothers and husbands, to wail for the dead, to grieve for the defenders who had been taken captive. The attackers had lost men, too. Red Crown warriors led some of the Moon warriors into the village as prisoners. Other Red Crown warriors helped the women to carry the wounded and the dead.

Soon, Nictay knew, those men would return across the field of battle and satisfy themselves that the invaders had not lingered in the jungle to set an ambush. Once they were sure that all the able-bodied Moon warriors had retreated, they would scour the jungle for stragglers like the one Nictay had found. But Nictay meant for the big, scarred Moon warrior to be *her* captive.

She whispered her apologies to the plants as she pulled off more leaves. "Forgive me, Her Daughter. My need is great. I thank you for what I must take." Then she hurried back to the tree where her Moon warrior sat with his obsidian-toothed club in his lap. Among his fresh wounds were traces of old ones; he had many white scars on his arms and legs, and one on his cheek. His nose had been broken some time in the past and healed crooked. His expression was so passive, his posture looked so relaxed that he seemed to be merely taking his ease. But his skin looked gray. He had lost a lot of blood.

"What is your name?" she asked.

"Do your priests care how their sacrifices are named?" His words came slowly, as if he were drunk on balche. But it was blood loss, no doubt. Nictay's words had been heavy in her mouth like that when she had bled herself, seeking a vision.

Nictay bound the leaves to his legs with cotton string. "I have already told you. I am not from this village. My people do not make sacrifice of their captives. Our gods demand only the sacrifice that they take themselves upon the sea. Fishermen drown, and the gods are satisfied." She gave him a water gourd. "Drink."

He sipped, watching her. "If you are not of these people," he said, "then they will think you are of mine." The water had helped. Words slipped more easily from his lips.

"I am not dressed as one of your women."

"No," he admitted, taking in the details of her plain cotton cloak, her shell necklace "But they will not stop to consider. It will not go well for you."

"That is why you must stand. We must get away from here."

"You saw my legs. Leave me! The gods have made their decision about me. Maker of Himself has decided." Breath whistled through his crooked nose.

"You are as good as dead if I leave you. And if I save you, your life is mine."

"The gods have decided."

"No god attacked you, but men. You fought well. Swinging your great club, wearing your feathered helmet...how great a prize you seemed! That is why so many tried for you. Now stand."

"But my legs…"

"The Red Crowns cut you many times, yes, but they did not sever the tendons. Up!" She picked up her spear, then strained to lift him. He made no effort to stand.

"Why should I go with you?"

"Because you'll die if you stay!"

"If I'm to save myself, let me crawl after my own men."

"I need you."

His gaze on her was hard, speculative. "Need me for what?"

Nictay pursed her lips. She could tell him the truth, but the trials of her village meant nothing to foreigners. Once again, she would have to lie.

"Come with me, and I will make you a rich and powerful noble."

He grimaced. "I am a Nacom of the Moon People. Would you make me greater than that?"

So he was indeed a great warrior. A veteran. A general. He was just what she was looking for. "I would make you a rival to the greatest Nacoms of the Middle People," she said. "That jade you wear on your breast plate, the feathers of your helmet are nothing compared to the wealth my people take from the sea."

The warrior grunted. "Who are you to offer these things?"

"I am a princess."

The sound he made was like soft laughter, but bitter. "You haven't the look of nobility."

"Our customs are not like yours," she said, "and I do not travel in my regalia. Why should I call attention to myself?"

"A woman alone is of interest whether she is high or low," he said.

"And so I have come here by stealth. Will you quibble with me until the Red Crowns come? Stand! I have need of a warrior like you." She strained again to lift him.

Shakily, he rose. He said, "There is no honor in bleeding to death in the jungle, Shell Woman."

"You will be honored among my people. Alive."

"As if I could walk all the way to the sea. I don't have that many steps in my legs."

"Take one," she said.

Leaning against her, he took a step, trembling. He mad a bitter face, as if embarrassed by his weakness. She had been about to offer to carry his club, but thought better of it.

"Another step now," she said, looking over her shoulder toward the village. "And another."

"Caan Cuy," he said. "My name is Caan Cuy."

"I am called Nictay," she said. "The Princess Nictay."

At home, her grandmother had warned her about lies. Shaking a half-shucked corncob at her granddaughter, she had said, "One day you will reap a harvest from them that you do not expect." But how could Nictay fulfill the tasks that her visions set for her except by lying? Foreigners would not want to give her willingly what she sought when she ventured into enemy lands to spy. So she had pretended to be a trader from a non-existent city, a representative of a noble, offering cacao on terms that were *almost* too good to be true. Greed made the enemy merchants eager to offer her protection and information. They gave her gifts of city clothes, and she ended up looking more and more like who she pretended to be. She had lied her way to the valley of the Middle People, had seen their Island City in the center of a mountain lake. She had seen how powerful they really were. And she had learned that the Middle People had overrun and destroyed villages and even whole cities that opposed them.

When she first learned this, when she first confirmed the ferocity of the Middle People, she despaired. Not long ago, Nictay's village had never even heard of the Middle People. Now, because of the Middle People raiders, Nictay's people had been forced to take refuge on an island off the coast, but without fresh water, the island was no place to settle for good. Were Nictay's people to be extinguished by this new enemy?

But Nictay had learned of more than the Middle People's ferocity. She had discovered something that gave her hope. The Middle People did not sack all the villages and cities they warred against. Many people *were* driven from their ancestral lands, never to return. But the Middle People respected enemies who fought as they did, who traded captives in battle. If her people could learn these foreign ways, they might negotiate, if not peace, a sustainable enmity that would let them return to their own lands. The only costs would be some tribute, perhaps fish, and the obligation to fight the Middle People now and then in flower wars, losing a few villagers as captives for sacrifice. This was better than annihilation.

How could her people learn to fight Flower Wars, those ritual battles to exchange captives? The obsidian toothed war clubs were unknown to Nictay's village until the first Middle People raiders had come. Nictay's people fought and hunted with spears. They did not know how to block and attack with a shield, how to slash at an enemy's legs and take a captive. They didn't know how to fix the obsidian points into the club's flat blade, like teeth in a shark's jaw.

Certain that she must discover how to teach these new ways, Nictay returned to her village. She bled herself and fasted for a vision.

Then the First Mother has shown her the path she must walk. She must take a captive. Not one of the Middle People, but a warrior who fought like them. She must bring home a master of the obsidian club, some fighter from the southern peoples: the Jaguar Tails, the Red Crowns, the Dog Eaters. Or a Moon warrior, a man like Caan Cuy.

So it was that she had crossed jungle alone. She had seen a war party leaving the Moon city, and she had followed them to the Red Crown Village. Hidden in the jungle, she watched the battle unfold. Caan Cuy was brilliant, cutting at the legs of his enemies with the black teeth of his club, knocking them down with his shield. He might have taken many captives had the Red Crowns not ganged up on him.

It had all gone perfectly. Caan Cuy, her captive, a teacher for her people, had been wounded just enough to be left behind, but not so badly that she had no chance of saving him. He would be the teacher her village required.

They were slow. Caan Cuy's legs stiffened on the second day, and he took even shorter, shakier steps. Then the rains came. Water fell in torrents through the canopy. Big drops pelted their skin like pebbles wherever they crossed a clearing open to the sky. In places, the mud was slick and greasy. In others, it was watery and sucked at their feet.

From time to time, she noticed that he would look toward the south as if considering a return to his own people. She would make up stories, then, of the riches that her father bestowed on warriors. She did not worry yet what Caan Cuy would do once he learned that her father was a simple fisherman, that there was no emperor among her people. What would he say when he found no stone palaces, when he saw that the only riches were in fish and fruit and shells? She would deal with that later. What mattered was getting him back to her people, pressing him closer to them and farther from the Moon city.

On the third day, Caan Cuy's fever began. He stopped often to stare through the rain-grayed air, as if he saw enemies where there were only more trees.

They were hungry all the time. Nictay could not leave Caan Cuy to hunt for fear that she would not find him again. She crushed ants with her fingers. They were sour, and it took so long to gather them that they were hardly better than nothing.

In the middle of the fourth rain-soaked night, Caan Cuy groaned out, "Water!" He waved his hands before his face.

"Water!"

In the darkness, Nictay groped for the gourd. She brought it to him, but he pushed it away and said, "Too much water!" She made him drink anyway, and once he had taken a swallow, he drank eagerly. Then his hands flailed again against the rain. "Too much water!"

His fever made him careless. The next day, he just missed stepping on a yellowjaw serpent. Later, clumsy with exhaustion and walking ahead of Nictay, he stumbled and fell face-first into a pool. He had mistaken a mat of water lilies for solid ground. When he got his feet beneath him, he stared at the logs in the pool that moved toward him. But they weren't logs. Crocodiles. Still he stood watching until Nictay had splashed in beside him to pull him back to solid ground.

His wounds no longer bled. Nonetheless, every day a little more of his strength left him, a little more of his wits drained away. When he dropped his obsidian-toothed club for the third time, Nictay picked it up and carried it herself.

"Sleep," Nictay encouraged him at the end of the fifth day. "Soon you will be among new friends."

She awoke to hear the whistling of his breath, which reassured her. But something was wrong. In the bluish phosphorescent light of the jungle, she saw black flowers blooming from Caan Cuy's sandaled feet and her own hand. As she puzzled at them and willed herself to alertness, she felt the wetness on her hand, the faintest tickle of a tiny tongue. A bat. She closed her hand around it and flung it away. When she rose, the bats feeding on Caan Cuy flew off.

That was when she heard the nearby cough of a jaguar. Was it stalking them? She spent the rest of that night wide awake, listening, knowing that a spear was little discouragement to a hungry jaguar, but unwilling to resign herself to the cat's mercy, unwilling to sleep.

✦ ✦ ✦

In the morning, the rain continued, and Caan Cuy could not rise. Nictay yanked on his arms to drag him, inches at a time, through the mud to the base of a tree where he could sit up, leaning against the black trunk. She removed the leaves that bound his wounds and decided not the replace them when she saw the moldy splotches on his skin. The warrior's eyes were glassy. Sweat beaded on his lips.

"We will rest today," Nictay said, kneeling beside him.

Caan Cuy grinned at her, or grimaced. It was hard to tell. He let his head drop back against the tree trunk. An ant crawled close to his eye, but he made no effort to sweep it away.

They were still many days from the coast. "I would leave you and go for help, if we were nearer."

The moon warrior shut his eyes. "I am dying," he said.

"No!" Nictay pinched his chest, hard. He did not flinch or open his eyes. "You will live!" But she knew that as long as they lingered in the jungle rains, he would only get weaker. "Do you hear?" she shouted very close to his ear. "You will not die! I need you!" But what would he care about what she or her village needed? "You will not die!"

Caan Cuy did not move. He made no sound.

"I am a princess!" she shouted. "Great honors await you!" She shook him. "I forbid you to die!"

Laughter. Nictay held herself very still. She heard a woman's laughter nearby. Where was it coming from? Nictay looked around. She saw nothing but leaves and vines. The voice seemed to come from in front as much as behind, from the left as much as the right, below as much as above.

The shells of Nictay's necklace rattled as she jumped to her feet. "Who's there? Show yourself!"

The laughter continued, then ceased. "Who am I?" asked a womanly voice, neither young nor old. "Why do you not tell me instead who you are. Who trespasses at my front door?"

Trespass? Front door? There was nothing here but dense jungle, as far as Nictay could tell. But if she had truly trespassed, then a show of righteous confidence might be best. Nictay stood up straight. "I am the Princess Nictay," she said. She remembered what Caan Cuy had called her. Shell Woman. "Princess Nictay of the Shell Woman clan," she elaborated. "If you have aid to offer, I would thank you to show yourself and offer it. If not, I would thank you to leave us."

"Ah, a princess," said the voice. "But why is your head shaped like a commoner's? You don't have the look of nobility."

"Among my people," Nictay said, "no mother shapes her child's head." That much, at least, was true. Nictay's village was small. There were no nobles among them.

"And this man?" asked the voice. "Why does his head have a noble shape?"

"He was once from a band of foreigners who have been adopted into my clan."

"Why do you forbid him even the respite of death?"

"He is a great fighter," Nictay said, then added, "He is my general. I need him. He is Nacom Caan Cuy, leader of the shark warriors, captor of men, slayer of enemies."

"Yet *you* carry the war club."

"Women are warriors among my people," Nictay invented. "We are captors of souls on the battlefield as well as in our houses. We know the pains of both battle and childbirth."

"I had not known there were such people," said the voice with a touch of mockery.

"Not heard of us? Not heard of the…the Highlands People? We are the greatest rivals to the Middle People. We are their closest enemy, and we are their match. Or haven't you heard of the Middle People, either?"

"I know about them," said the voice. The jungle around Nictay had been dark already, but now the gloom deepened.

"I know about the Middle People. But you Highlands People…" There was mirth in the voice. "…you were unknown to me. Until now." Nictay felt the ground tremble. The tree trunk that Caan Cuy was propped against seemed to swell, then flatten out against Caan Cuy's back. The high canopy overhead receded, as if the whole jungle were growing taller, as if the sky were receding, or as if the ground where Nictay stood were sinking. Vines and ferns shrank back into the ground, leaving it barren.

"What is happening?"

The voice gave no answer. Nictay was sure now that she was dropping, that the ground where she stood was sinking deep into the earth. The last gray light dimmed to blackness, and still the ground trembled. When it stopped, the air was still. No rain fell. No insects churred. No night birds sang. And the blackness was absolute, without the blue phosphorescent glow of decaying wood or the green sparks of fireflies.

Caan Cuy breathed. Nictay heard her own heart beating. That was all.

Nictay knew now that the voice had been the voice of a goddess. She knew she should have spoken with more respect. Honesty would have served better than lies, though now that she had told such an inventive lie, she could hardly take it back. The goddess had seemed amused by what Nictay had said, and the truth now might anger her. If she was not already angry. Who can guess at the thoughts of the gods?

"Lady," Nictay said, kneeling though she didn't know if even a goddess could see in such gloom. In utter blackness, even a jaguar might be blind. "Lady, if I have given some offense, I am sorry. I did not know you. I did not understand your nature." Her voice echoed.

No answer came.

The ground under Nictay's knees was hard. She felt it with her fingertips, rapped it with her knuckles. It was not mud, or even hard-packed earth, but cold unyielding stone. "Lady," Nictay said, "if it is shelter that you grant us, I thank you."

Again, silence.

Nictay had carried no fire, or any means to start one. And now even if she could strike a spark, what could she use for fuel?

She stood. She waved Caan Cuy's overhead. The ceiling, if there was one, was out of reach. Was this a cave? There might be drop-offs that she couldn't see. She inched forward, tapping the stone floors with her toes before she shifted her weight. She waved the club before her, flinching when at last it grazed something solid. A wall. She felt it with her other hand. The wall was flat, with regular seams where great blocks of stone fit together. It was a made wall. This was not a cave, but a stone house or temple like the city peoples built.

Gingerly, she felt her way along the wall. It extended for a long distance without interruption, and when Nictay could no longer hear Caan Cuy's breathing, she went back to him.

"Caan Cuy?" She found his form in the blackness and nudged him. He did not stir, but his breathing was regular and strong. She groped for the water gourd, poured a few drops past his lips, then groped about again. There was another wall opposite the first. She followed it in both directions, returning again when she could no longer hear Caan Cuy's whistling breath.

She went back to him once more, tried again to rouse him. He groaned but did not awaken. She felt his neck. The fever had broken. Now if they did not die of thirst or starvation, he might live after all. She sat beside him in the blackness. At least here she did not think there were bats or jaguars. Here she might sleep in peace.

She dreamed many times of waking, of taking a narrow stairway back to the surface of the world. Then she woke to find herself still in the darkness. Or did she dream that, too?

Were all her awakenings also dreams? At last she opened her eyes to orange light. Flames burned steadily against the high walls, far above her. She moved, and felt stiff as if from a week of sleeping. Her eyes were so dry, so crusted with sleep that it hurt to blink. Her tongue felt swollen, her throat papery. The pressure of her bladder was so painful, though, that she didn't need to thump her breastbone to see if she were truly awake. She exhaled what would have been a groan if her throat were not so dry, and she sat up.

"There's water," said Caan Cuy. He was sitting with his back to the wall. Light danced in his dark eyes. "And food."

She looked to where he pointed. Three water jugs and two bowls of fruit were against the wall. There were breadnuts, too, and palm hearts. Next to these was a shallow basin for washing. There was even a chamber pot.

"Someone's looking out for us," Caan Cuy said. "But who? Where are we? I don't remember coming here."

Nictay held her hand up to silence him. She drank from one of the jars, then took the pot down the corridor, beyond where the last flames curled up from the walls. In the half-darkness, she relieved herself. Leaving the pot behind, she returned to Caan Cuy, knelt beside the basin, and washed her shaking hands. She tore the yellow rind of a guava with her teeth and swallowed the pink flesh. She devoured a second one. A third. Then she sighed, far from satisfied, but no longer desperate. She looked at Caan Cuy. "We are guests," she said. "Or prisoners. I do not know which." She told him how they had come there, though she did not mention how she had lied to the goddess.

"I might have guessed a Power's hand was in this," Caan Cuy said. "Those are no ordinary lamps." He nodded toward the flames that curled out from the walls. "I see no wick, no channel for oil. The stone itself seems to burn."

"You seem…better."

"I am healed." He slapped the scars where his wounds had been. "We slept a long time. And she restored my strength. She knit my wounds." He looked at the walls. They seemed to rise forever. The ceiling was so high that the orange glow of the flames did not reach it, if there were a ceiling at all. "What can she want from us?"

"So very little," said a voice that seemed to emerge from the walls.

Caan Cuy sat up very straight. Nictay looked around, though naturally the goddess did not reveal herself. "I desire only that you should entertain me. Princess, you say that women are warriors as much as the men among the Highland People."

Nictay exchanged a glance with Caan Cuy. "That is what I told you, Lady."

Caan Cuy frowned.

"And if you are such close neighbors to the Middle People, you must surely play the ball game as they do."

Nictay had seen the ball courts of the Middle People. The game they played there was known, in different forms, to all the city peoples. She nodded, though she had never played the game herself, nor heard of any woman who did.

"And your general? Speak to me, Nacom Caan Cuy of the Shell Clan."

"I am of the Swallow Clan," said Caan Cuy.

"You *were* of that clan," Nictay said, "until my people adopted you."

Caan Cuy considered her, eyes narrowed.

"I play the ball game," he said.

"Then you both shall play for me," said the voice of the Power. "You will play to the sacred count. Each point shall add a day, beginning with the day after One Deer. The first player to rest again on One Deer shall return home to the city of the Highland People…"

"The city of Highland People?" Caan Cuy said. "I have never heard of such a place!"

Nictay pleaded with her eyes, but the Moon warrior said, "Lady, when I win, you must return me to the Moon city. That is my home."

After a moment, the voice said, "And you, *Princess* Nictay. What is your true home? For there are no Highland People, no great rivals to the Middle People. And you are no noble. Where, truly, are you from?"

Nictay bowed her head. "From a village by the sea. It is called Kana's Place."

"Did you think you could deceive me? I am the first born of earth and sky. My ear is everywhere. There are no peoples I have not heard of. You have never stepped into a ball court, have you? But you are in one now, and you play for your life." At these words, the corridor changed shape, growing wider where they stood. Walls formed at either end, with smaller chambers perpendicular to the first: an I-shaped court. "Choose your ends," said the voice. "Then prepare. The winner returns home. The loser dies to honor me."

Caan Cuy considered the court for a moment, then walked to one end. Nictay went to the opposite end. In the smaller, back-court chamber, she found leather guards for her forearms and shins. She tied them on, not certain that she was doing it right, and remembered what she could of the rules. They traded serves. The served ball must bounce on the server's own side no more than once...

She tied on the yoke that would protect her hips. Her grandmother had been right about lies. But how could Nictay have done otherwise? Would she have lied to a goddess, knowing she was a goddess? Of course not! She would not have lied to anyone at all if honest appeals could have done her any good in foreign lands. She had been a powerless woman among a powerless people. She'd been using her wits because her wits were all she had.

What were the chances that she could beat a warrior who had practiced at this game? How could she use her wits in a game that depended instead on strength?

The voice of the goddess said, "From One Deer, I advance you both to Two Yellow. The rest of the points you must earn. Begin!"

Nictay strode to her side of the court. Caan Cuy stood in his back chamber. He held a ball. He said, "I am grateful to you, Shell Woman, for saving me. I give you my thanks. But we are enemies now."

"I want to live as much as you do," Nictay said. "But we are not enemies."

"Begin!" said the goddess.

Caan Cuy threw the ball. It bounced in his court, in Nictay's court, and skipped toward the back chamber. Nictay lunged at it, swinging her arm through the empty air. As she landed, she knocked over a marker stone. The ball bounced into the back chamber.

"A point for the chamber and a point for the stone," said the goddess. "Caan Cuy's count is Four Dog."

Nictay got up slowly, rubbing her shoulder. She returned the marker stone to its position and retrieved the ash-colored rubber ball. She squeezed it in her hand. How hard must she throw it to get it to bounce in the right way?

Nictay threw. The ball bounced twice on her own side.

"Caan Cuy's count is Five Monkey," said the goddess. "Nictay remains at Two Yellow."

By the time Nictay made her first successful serve, Caan Cuy's score had run the course of twenty day names and stood at Eight Deer. On the rare occasions when she returned the ball, Caan Cuy always knocked it back to her side where it often died before she could reach it. He never ran into his own marker stones. Nictay, on the other hand, concentrated so hard on returns that she often knocked her own stones down. Caan

Cuy even scored by hitting her marker stones with the ball. By the time she got one serve past him to advance to Three Thunder, he had run through the twenty day names again, resting on Two Deer and Nine Deer on the way to One Tooth.

At this rate, he would cycle through the 260 sacred days before Nictay had even reached 13 Rain.

It was hot. Nictay's skin was slippery under the leather guards. Her throat burned.

When her turn came to serve, she held the ball.

"Throw," said the goddess.

"I thirst."

"Warriors do not stop to drink in the midst of battle," the goddess chided.

"And we fight a battle through a year of day names. Would you keep us from resting through a whole year? Give us drink."

"Throw."

"He scores two and three points at a time. Is the outcome in question? Only let me slake my thirst before I die."

From his side, Caan Cuy called out, "No food, no drink, no rest until the game rests again at One Deer. That is the nature of the game."

"Throw," said the goddess. "Thirst will drive you to finish the game. March to your water jug, warrior, though there is death at its bottom. Throw."

So Nictay threw. Caan Cuy returned with his hip. Nictay ran to meet the ball, tripped on a marker, and struck the ball with her hand. "A point for touching with the hand. A point for the marker. From One Tooth, Caan Cuy leaps to Three Jaguar."

Then Nictay saw it, the way out of this game. And she laughed bitterly, for it was a dangerous way, one that the goddess had surely understood from the start.

Nictay played a little better as the game continued. She became more aware of the placement of the marker stones, and more of the balls she slapped with her hips or kicked with her shins went where she wanted them to go. She had advanced all the way to Six Dog when Caan Cuy scored the point that brought him to One Jaguar and began the final count toward One Deer. He scored the next point, then the next.

It was Caan Cuy's turn to serve. The Nacom had not spoken since many serves ago. Now he said, "I cannot lose, Nictay, yet you continue to play with determination. You are a proud woman."

"She is a liar," said the voice of the goddess.

"I knew that from the start," said Caan Cuy. "But I salute her even so." And he bowed to Nictay.

"You say you cannot lose," Nictay said. "Have you also considered that you cannot win? I play for my life, Caan Cuy. Do you think I will surrender it lightly?"

"It is not a matter of surrender," Caan Cuy said, and served the ball. Nictay made no attempt to return it. The ball bounced in his court, in hers, and into the back chamber.

"Point for Caan Cuy. He rests at Four Thought."

"You need eleven points to rest at One Deer," Nictay said. "I make you a gift of this one." She hurled the ball hard. It passed all the way into Caan Cuy's back chamber, striking the wall.

"Point for Caan Cuy," said the goddess. "He rests at Five Blade."

"Why did you do that?"

"Don't you understand yet, Nacom?" Nictay said. "This is the game that neither of us is meant to win. This game is for the goddess's pleasure, and it is a bitter delight she takes."

"I do not understand."

"Serve," said the goddess. "Do you not thirst? Serve and bring the game to a close."

Caan Cuy threw the ball. Nictay rushed to meet it, caught it in her hand and kicked over a marker stone at the same time. "One point for touching, one for the stone," said the goddess. "Caan Cuy stands at Seven Marksman."

"A few more points," Nictay said. She threw the ball into Caan Cuy's back chamber again. "That gives you Eight Lefthanded."

Caan Cuy served again. Nictay knocked over a marker stone before the ball had even come to her side, and she kicked another stone as the ball passed through her court.

"On point for the back chamber, two for the stones," said the goddess. "Caan Cuy rests at Twelve Snake."

"Do you see it now?" Nictay asked. She served into the back chamber again, giving up another point. She still rested at Six Dog, not yet halfway through the count. Caan Cuy was at Thirteen Death, only a point from victory. But he couldn't win. "We play not to surpass a certain score, but to *rest* there."

Caan Cuy held the ball, considering.

"It is true that I lied to you," Nictay said. "I am no princess. But my people need a warrior like you. That much is true. I would have said anything at all to keep you from despairing, to encourage you to come with me rather than die in the jungle. I lied, but with good reason. And it is for that reason that I will not lose this game. Nor will I let you win it. I must live to return to my people. I must bring you with me."

"That is not possible. The bargain of the goddess…"

"Serve!" cried the goddess's voice. Caan Cuy threw. His serve was good, and as it passed by, Nictay knocked over a stone.

"Two points," said the goddess, laughing. "Caan Cuy skips One Deer and rests at Two Yellow."

"This is her game," said Nictay, "to deny us food or drink or rest as long as we play. And how long will be play? When either of us has the power to keep the other's score from ever resting on One Deer, just how long will we keep this up?"

"We will play until we are too weak to play," Caan Cuy said, nodding. "We will play until we die of thirst."

"There is another way," Nictay said. "But you must trust me."

"She is a liar," said the goddess. "You know this about her already, Nacom."

"I must live, and I must keep you alive," said Nictay. "Liar or not, you can trust me more than I can trust you. I need you. You do not need me."

"Tell me," said Caan Cuy. "I will consider."

So it was that exhausted, they played on. Caan Cuy deliberately knocked over his own markers, as Nictay knocked over her own. It took a long time for them to tie the score, and all the while the voice of the goddess reminded Caan Cuy that Nictay was untrustworthy. At the same time, she told Nictay to consider whether Caan Cuy would ever go with her back to her village. Clearly, what he wanted was to return to his own people, not serve hers.

When the score stood at Thirteen Death for each of them, it was Nictay's serve. Her papery throat burned when she asked, "Will you trust me, Nacom Caan Cuy of the Moon People?"

"You cannot," said the goddess.

Across the court, he met her eyes. "I will."

"She is a liar."

"And I will trust you, Caan Cuy. Just have a care. No not trip over a stone as the ball sails by."

"He will betray you."

He sat down. "Satisfied?"

He was an agile man. Even from where he sat, he might jump up and topple a stone in time, giving her two points, sending her past One Deer the way she had done it to him. But she had to trust him. There was no other way.

She took careful aim so that she wouldn't strike one of his markers with the ball. She served.

The ball bounced in her court. In his.

It sailed toward the back chamber. Caan Cuy sat, arms folded.

Nictay knocked over one of her own stones.

"A point for the chamber," growled the goddess. "A point for the stone. Each of you rests at One Deer."

"Water," said Caan Cuy. "You promised."

A water jug appeared in the center of the court. Caan Cuy and Nictay met there. Each took a swallow, then Caan Cuy said, "Drink. Slake your thirst. You discovered the way home for both of us."

"She did," said the goddess as Nictay drank. "But as you ended the game in a way I did not intend, so shall I honor my pledge to you in a way that *you* did not intend." And before Nictay had finished drinking, the flames in the walls died. They were in utter blackness.

Light, barely perceptible and gray, grew around them. Gradually, the gloom lifted and they found themselves on a hillside. Rain fell on their faces. The water jug was still in Nictay's hands.

"Your clothes!" Caan Cuy said. He himself was dressed as he had always been, except that he no longer wore the yoke and pads of a ball player.

Nictay looked down at herself. She wore a cape of red and green feathers. There were sandals on her feet, and an enormous jade pendant hung down between her breasts.

Caan Cuy's obsidian-toothed war club lay on the ground near his feet. On the ground at Nictay's feet was another one just like it. The rain began to slacken.

"Princess," said a man who had been standing behind them. They both turned, startled. "Have we not rested enough? Your father awaits us."

"Ahkbal?" said Caan Cuy. "My brother?" He stepped forward to clasp the man's hand. "You are here?"

Ahkbal looked at him strangely. "I have never left, Nacom." He peered into Caan Cuy's face. "Are you ill? Is the fever still with you?"

Caan Cuy looked at Nictay, who had no assurance to offer. "I am—" Caan Cuy started. He shrugged. "I am all right."

"Princess?" said Ahkbal.

"Lead the way," she said. He gave her the same strange look, but he took the lead on the mountain path that brought them to the top of a ridge. On a ledge below, Nictay saw a party of nobles standing and watching the valley below. She gasped, and then looking into the valley, she froze.

Caan Cuy took her arm. "What?"

She nodded at the ledge. "My father," she said. "He is a fisherman, but there he stands among men of noble dress. Look at his robes! They are the clothes of a great man!"

"Of an emperor," Caan Cuy agreed.

"Princess?" said Ahkbal. "Is something wrong?"

Nictay stood up as straight as she could. In what she hoped would sound like the tones of a princess, she said, "Go ahead and announce us."

He bowed and left them.

"So that is what she meant," Nictay said. "She sent us home, but not to *our* homes."

"Some of the emperor's body guards are women. I know some of them. Women of the Moon city. But women never carried clubs and shields in my country!"

"Mittat!" Nictay said, recognizing a friend. But what was Mittat doing in the robes of a warrior?

"Is this place…?"

"This is the valley of the middle people," Nictay said. "But that city below us…" She looked again at the palace, the temple pyramids, the houses of nobles, the huts, the surrounding fields. "I don't know it. I never saw it before."

"What can it be," Caan Cuy said, understanding now, "but the city of the Highland People?" He pointed out onto the plain between the highland city and the island city of the Middle People. Great rows of warriors lined up to face one another.

Their feathered robes and painted shields were brilliant even at this distance, even under a gray sky. "Flower War."

"She gave us the home of my lie," Nictay said. "I wanted my people to be the equals of the Middle People."

"So it seems they are," Caan Cuy said. And with bitterness, he added, "Now they are my people, too. And yours are mine. I see priests of the Moon city attending your father down there. Your father, the emperor. And how many of my friends and yours will die down there today, women as well as men, in this flower war of your making? In this world of your lie?"

She gave him a hard look. "I did what I had to do for my people, Nacom Caan Cuy, my general."

He looked away from her.

"Come," she said. "We have our lives. We have our new lives."

He met her gaze again.

"My father awaits us, Nacom." She nodded towards the ledge where the nobles watched the flower war unfold. "Let us go to him. Let us discover what sort of world we have made."

She started down the path. And Caan Cuy, taking in a deep breath through his crooked nose, followed her.

Printed in the United States
99170LV00001B/10/A